CW00860117

The Xaros Reckoning

The Ember War Saga Book 9

Richard Fox

Copyright © 2016 Author Name

All rights reserved.

ISBN: 1540663035
ISBN-13: 978-1540663030

For Sharon,
Whose touch is on every page

CHAPTER 1

Keeper watched a solar system die. His drone armada swept across a terraformed moon orbiting a gas giant and into the deep caverns once inhabited by over nine billion Vishrakath. The final pockets of resistance would fall in the next hour. He reached out to the drones and directed some of their number toward vaults hidden within the planet's other rocky moons where a vast number of juvenile Vishrakath and egg layers had attempted to hide.

He knew of the General's methods: annihilate all armed resistance before scouring away the populace at leisure, but Keeper had a different opponent to defeat first.

Hope.

Keeper turned his attention to a battle raging above the fifth planet, an icy world at the far edge of the system's habitable zone. Millions of Xaros drones battled a Vishrakath fleet that once numbered in the tens of thousands. Now, crashed hulks scarred the planet's glaciers and the defenders struggled with but a few hundred vessels.

The Xaros master picked out a Vishrakath battleship and ordered his drones to dispose of the ship's crew, but to seize it intact.

+You're wasting time.+ The Engineer appeared in the void next to him, the other Xaros Master taking the form of an ever-draining hourglass. +Malal is here or he is not. Let the drones do their work. They know what they're looking for.+

+Your drones are such crude instruments. They will destroy any form or trace of living intelligence—that includes Malal.+ Keeper looked to the Vishrakath home world. The surface was expansive jungles with wide polar caps. The entrance to subterranean cities boasted energy cannons and many hangars for their void fighters. Orbital stations guarded the high orbit, each built around a massive laser. The Vishrakath would resist. Keeper estimated the planet would fall within three day cycles, unless he brought in more drones. The loss of scores of drones meant nothing, not when he could fabricate more by the billion.

+I designed their intelligence matrix. They will not harm our prize,+ the Engineer said. +You tarry. Unleash the rest of the force and be done with this. Being in the presence of a failed species sickens me.+

+Finesse was never your strength. The Vishrakath were prepared for us. Their information network was scuttled. The drones have found nothing but books bound in polymers, quaint. If Malal is here, he only just arrived. If he isn't, there will be no record for us to find and aid our search.+

+The logical conclusion to your scenario is...vile.+

+We have already broken the prohibition against using wormhole technology. What is contact with a lesser species compared to that?+

The Engineer's form flipped upside down.

+There must be no record of any of this,+ the Engineer said. +If the Masters learn of this...+

+We can correct the record. Lay any blame at the feet of the General—not that he can complain or contest.+

The drones within the Vishrakath battleship signaled that the vessel had been seized and the crew annihilated. Keeper watched as the last of the fleet made a suicidal charge toward a drone leviathan. Disintegration beams lashed out and smashed the final ships into fragments.

+There. That should suffice.+ Keeper shifted into his photonic shell. +Care to partake? The experience may be informative.+

+No. You may sully yourself. I will not.+

+Yet you are eager to meet with Malal. Hypocrisy is unbecoming of our kind.+

The hourglass broke open and the grains of sand became a model of the Milky Way galaxy. Tiny runes appeared over stars, concentrated on the opposite side of the galaxy from the Vishrakath world.

+Malal's species once occupied much of the galaxy,+ the Engineer said. +I've examined some of their technology, but it will take time to gain a full understanding, and there are others who can complete the task faster once the Apex arrives. I am certain Malal's race ascended from this galaxy. They defeated the great void. They moved beyond death's reach. We almost had our own escape when the annihilation wave drove us out of our home. Malal can lead us to his answer.+

+You have no faith that we can answer the question on our own?+

+Why wait for immortality? The General's destruction proves we are vulnerable. If Malal has the solution, we must take it.+

+At least we agree on something.+ Keeper sped through the void to the captured Vishrakath ship. Metal strands crisscrossed the converted asteroid, running between weapons emplacements and docking bays. Keeper considered the unfinished surface of dust and craters that spoke of an aesthetic choice of the Vishrakath builders…or a sign of haste from a species railing against certain doom.

Keeper appeared on the ship's bridge. The polished rock walls bore tracks between the workstations on the walls, ceiling and deck. Xaros drones moved away from Keeper, their stalks high and charged in case the Vishrakath had left some sort of trap for their master. Keeper whisked the dusty remnants of the bridge crew away and willed a drone over to operate a communication station. Keeper shifted into an armored body, reminiscent of the General's preferred form.

The drone opened a channel to the Vishrakath home world, calling upon a certain member of the species.

Keeper absorbed more data from the invasion force as he waited. The outer system colonies had been eradicated, shipyards in the system's two asteroid belts destroyed, the defenders of the ice world dead. Keeper sent his armada toward the home world...then his hail was finally answered.

A curved screen rose from work station and a Vishrakath appeared. Wexil's bulbous head had nine eyes, all formed differently to take in much more of the energy spectrum than most species in the galaxy.

Ivory-colored segmented legs stretched from his thorax and abdomen. The glowing eyes of onlookers filled the space behind Wexil.

"On behalf of the Vishrakath Imperium, we offer our unconditional surrender. Please, spare us. We will serve you in any matter you choose...just let us survive."

Keeper ordered the armada advancing toward the last surviving world to slow down and then held up a hand. Dust from the Vishrakath remains swirled into his hand and formed a diorama. A silent loop of Wexil and Malal speaking on Bastion played.

"I've had contact with Malal," Wexil said.

The dust reformed into a perfect replica of Wexil's home world. Yellow dots pinged from each of the subterranean cities.

"Malal...is not here."

Keeper crushed the world in his grasp.

"But I know where to find him! Please, I will tell you, but I ask you to promise to let us live."

Keeper sent the armada toward Wexil at full speed.

Two of Wexil's eyes darted aside, no doubt learning that the Xaros advance had begun again.

"The Qa'Resh took Malal. Along with the human ambassador, Stacey Ibarra. Qa'Resh'Ta vanished, jumped through a wormhole. They went back to Earth—I'm certain of it."

Earth. Where the General perished. Where the entire Xaros force sent to destroy the humans must have been destroyed. There was only one place in the galaxy that Keeper feared to tread, and it was Earth.

Keeper directed a deep scan of the Vishrakath world and found a fluctuation in quantum space hidden deep within the planet: a dome-shaped vessel with a jump engine. Keeper created a new diorama in his hand. The dome ship left the planet and went straight into the system's star. The diorama shifted back to the home world, then to the ship jumping away. Drones swarmed over the planet.

"You want us to destroy our jump engine. As you wish. Let us unload the children and eggs aboard and we will do so at once."

Keeper brought up a timer, just enough for the jump ship to reach the sun if it left within the next few minutes. The drones overwhelmed the world again.

"As you wish." Wexil's eyes went pale. Keeper did not care to learn the Vishrakath's body language. He needed nothing but their immediate compliance.

Keeper ordered the armada back to the ice world and directed his drones aboard the Vishrakath ship to send it on a collision course to the surface. He morphed out of his armor and returned to the Engineer.

+They cooperated. Malal is—+

+I listened. Curiosity got the better of me. Destroy them. Now.+

+They cannot answer questions if they are all dead. The drones will remain and construct a Crucible over this world. We have our next target: Earth. Once we have Malal, we will cleanse this system...and the rest of the galaxy.+

CHAPTER 2

Across the wall of the Marine rec room, a holo of the *Breitenfeld* soared through the vastness of space, trailed by the gargantuan *Canticle of Truth*. A crescendo of bombastic music filled the room as credits rolled up the screen.

Weiss jumped off a metal and plastic chair, clapping wildly.

"Woo! Gets better every time I see it." He snapped his fingers twice and the room's computer stopped the movie, *The Last Stand on Takeni*. Lights rose, illuminating several more Marines: Orozco, Egan, Bailey and Standish. The last sat hunched forward, his face buried in his hands. Orozco grinned

10

from ear to ear. Bailey shook her head slowly while Egan frowned, a finger pressed to his lips.

"I honestly can't believe none of you have ever seen that movie," Weiss said, rubbing his hands together quickly. "So many questions right now. OK, did Captain Hale really make that great speech on the walls of New Abhaile before the first banshee attack?"

"That never happened," Bailey said. "The boss spent most of his time trying to get the city's defenses organized, showing the Dotok which way to point their rifles."

"What?" Weiss tugged at the collar of his shirt, revealing a tattoo of flowing script. "You mean I have to get it changed?"

Standish groaned into his palms.

"Get it removed, chunderhead," Bailey said. "In case you haven't noticed, Hale doesn't waste time with big speeches before a battle. Cherries like you will be too scared to remember it when the shooting starts and salty old farts like me know hot air when we hear it."

"Didn't you all run through a burning forest

or something?" Egan asked. "I saw the repair logs on your armor, been meaning to ask about that."

"That happened," Orozco said. "Hale told us to button up and then went running into an inferno." He shifted in his seat. "My codpiece got knocked loose during the landing. I still feel the heat on my *huevos*."

"What about loading all the Dotok kids onto Mules when the banshees were coming over the walls?" Weiss asked, his face growing pale.

"Kind of happened," Bailey said, frowning, "but we did that way out in the boonies. Not the city."

"And Oro rescuing that little girl from the collapsing house?" Weiss began to take several short, quick breaths.

"No," Orozco said, shaking his head, "but let's watch that part again. I looked *good*."

"Franklin fighting with a banshee on the *Breit*?" Weiss asked.

"That was me!" Standish snapped to his feet, his hands balled in anger. "I was the one going hand to hand with those walking nightmares. I'm the one that carried those elderly Dotok up the Mule ramp. I'm the one that gave up his rations so the orphans could eat. I didn't make Franklin's 'for the good of all free people' little pep talk but I'll take credit for it. I can't believe they replaced me." He looked to the ceiling and pounded his fists against his chest. "Cheated out of my moment of glory!"

Weiss's breathing became high-pitched and strained as hyperventilation set it.

"It's all...a lie?" The young Marine backed into the holo wall and sank to the floor.

Bailey grabbed him by the back of his neck and shoved his head between his knees. She fanned him with her hand and rolled her eyes.

"It's a propaganda movie, pup. I watched the same kind of stuff growing up about the Chinese taking Darwin. All a whole bunch of feel-good crap," Bailey said.

"Wait a minute." Egan raised a hand. "What about that Torni...person? The one that found us on—"

"Bastards cut her out too!" Standish kicked a tray table, sending plates and mostly eaten food flipping through the air.

"Who?" Weiss looked up, his breathing more controlled.

"I was the last person to ever talk to her," Standish said. "She stayed back, gave up her tanks so we could get a few more women and children off world. God, I still haven't had a chance to talk to her since..." He stormed out the door, slamming it behind him for good measure.

"What's that all about?" Egan asked.

"I wasn't there," Orozco shrugged.

"I was bleeding to death in the back of a Mule when all that happened." Bailey's hand went to her side, touching the place where a hunk of shrapnel had ripped her open.

"What're we...supposed to do...now?" Weiss asked. He took a deep breath, then leaned against the wall. "You guys know everyone in the solar system's seen this movie?"

"I'm OK with it." Orozco took a data slate from a pocket and brought it to life with a swipe. "Especially that shower scene. I get almost a hundred e-mails a day from the ladies."

His eyes widened as he flipped the slate toward Egan.

"Good lord, she's naked," Egan averted his eyes. "You get a lot of those?"

Orozco answered with a greedy laugh.

From just beyond the door, Standish yelled, "It's bullshit!"

Orozco laughed harder.

"All right, lads," Bailey said, putting her hands on her hips, "we're all going to let this movie stay fair dinkum bollocks. Nobody gets on the telly and tries to set the record straight or a billion people will get their knickers twisted. Bad enough trying to deal with Weiss getting a peek behind the veil."

"Fine by me." Orozco swiped his screen to the right, frowned, swiped again and smiled.

"I'll have a chat with Standish," Bailey said.

The door to the rec room opened with a bang. Steuben, their executive officer, loomed in the doorway.

"Combatives training in nine minutes," the Karigole said, "everyone."

"But Steuben," Orozco said, "we just finished

overhauling our armor *and* servicing the Mule turrets."

"I allowed you one hundred seventy-seven minutes of leisure activity," Steuben said. "Perhaps I was too generous?"

The Marines grumbled as they left the rec room.

****

Captain Hale sat on a long bench within a Mule, staring past the open ramp to a ground car on the far end of the landing pad. Three figures clustered near the self-driving vehicle, which was little more than a pod on wheels. The sun broke through fast-moving clouds, stretching bands of light over the concrete expanse. Hale shifted against the bench, unused to both the Mule's personnel transport setup and wearing just his service fatigues.

In the past years, he'd been in Mules that had crashed, been shot down or dropped him onto a hot landing zone. The idea of a Mule taking him anywhere but the fires of combat felt unnatural. His hands opened and closed as he rolled his shoulders back, wishing for the feel of his power armor against his body.

Hale glanced at the clock on his forearm screen, then to the distant figures.

First Sergeant Cortaro stepped out of the doorway leading to the cockpit and walked over, carrying a greasy paper bag.

"Seems our wheels-up time got pushed back another twenty minutes." Cortaro sat next to his commander, opened the bag and fished out a hamburger in a red and white wrapper.

"Eat while they're fresh, sir."

Hale's nose took in the aroma of cooked meat as his mouth salivated.

"I'll wait until we're back on the ship. Make sure everyone's got some," Hale said.

"We've got almost a hundred more in the cooler—minus the five I had to give the flyboys to delay our departure. There's still more than enough for the company. Even Orozco can't eat that many." Cortaro shook the hamburger at Hale.

Hale looked at the offering out of the corner

of his eye then snatched it from the other Marine's hands. He ripped the wrapper away and took a huge bite.

"Tastes just like I remember," Hale said through a full mouth.

"Unchanged since 1948." Cortaro set the bag between him and Hale and started munching on his own burger. "I don't know and I don't care how or why Ibarra brought back some of the old restaurants. I'm just glad we've got a little piece of home again."

Hale wiped a bit of ketchup from the side of his mouth and took a deep, satisfied breath.

"Our Marines will love this," he said. "You think Standish will eat his or sell them?"

"Sell. That kid's never missed a chance to make a buck. I tell you what, sir, I used to finish off a half-dozen of these at a time after training maneuvers out near Twenty-Nine Palms. Nothing like these after weeks in the sun and sand eating tube mush and drinking my own purified piss. I've got a couple for Yarrow too. You think he'll like them?"

"What's not to like?" Hale squeezed the empty wrapper into a ball and tossed it into the bag.

He looked at the pile of burgers for a second, then took out another one.

"I don't think he's ever had this before—not really, since he's a proccie. You think Ibarra put the memory of what these taste like into his head?"

"Given the line we almost had to stand in to get these, I'd say all the proccies share some core memories," Hale said.

"Don't take this the wrong way, sir, but the next time we're in an hour-long line and someone recognizes you from that movie and offers to let you cut to the front, just take the opportunity."

"I ended up signing autographs for twenty minutes while you placed the order. This being-famous stuff will take some getting used to."

"Yeah, well, I've done a pretty good job of keeping you from screwing up too bad, but I'm not trained to navigate the fame business. You'll be on your own once this war's over." Cortaro gave his stomach a pat.

Hale looked back across the tarmac. Yarrow had Lilith and his daughter, Mary, in an embrace. The captain tapped his fingertips against his lap.

"You thinking about leaving him behind?" Cortaro asked.

"No!" Hale snapped. "No...just because he's the only one on the *Breitenfeld* with a family. The only one with a ch—" Hale shut his mouth.

"With a child. I get it, sir. My wife and kids are with God." Cortaro crossed himself. "That's how it is now. How it is for everyone since the Xaros came. But I look over there and I see hope for what we could have in the future. People having families again. It sucks having to take him away from that. Poor Yarrow's got to explain that he'll be back soon and in one piece."

"That's not a promise he or I can keep," Hale said. "Best way we can guarantee that little family will continue is to transfer him dirt side. I can't do that— won't be fair to the rest of the team. Wait...did he ask for that?"

"No, sir, he knows his duty. He's been with us since Anthalas, lockstep through having that Malal devil in his head, finding out he's a proccie and every mess since then. Esprit de corps is a strong bond, but family is stronger. Yarrow understands that what we're doing ultimately keeps his family safe. I know that feeling he's got right now. It's like a cold stone in his gut. Never goes away until you get back home again."

Hale crossed his arms over his chest. "This next mission is more dangerous than anything we've done before. We leave him back and maybe there's one less widow. One less child that never had the chance to be raised by her father."

"So you're considering it?"

Hale set one ankle atop another. "I didn't say that."

"It's alright, sir. Means we're more to you than just warm bodies to be thrown into the breach. I knew those captain's bars wouldn't ruin you. You're in a shitty position. Take him back with us and what will that mean for his family? Leave him behind and what'll that mean for us if we lose our best corpsman? That's why you get paid the big bucks."

"I hate leaving people behind, no matter the situation. Torni. Rohen. I hate losing Marines too..."

"You can do everything right and still get killed. That's just war, sir. Here he comes."

Yarrow walked toward the Mule, a slight limp to his step. Hale heard a little girl sobbing.

"I hate this part," Hale said quietly.

"We all do. Maybe peace will break out once this is over and this'll be the last time we have to do this." Cortaro banged a fist against the bulkhead. The Mule's engines whined to life a few seconds later.

Yarrow came up the ramp and sat across from Hale. The corpsman wiped a sleeve across his eyes.

"Yarrow," Hale said over the rising engines. He waited until the young Marine looked up at him. "I'm going to bring you home, understand?"

A smile spread across Yarrow's face. "Sir, in case you haven't been keeping score, I'm normally the one that has to bring *you* home."

He looked back across the tarmac to his family as the ramp closed.

"Hey, catch." Cortaro took a burger out of the bag and tossed it to Yarrow.

CHAPTER 3

Caas and Ar'ri walked down a maintenance hallway buried beneath Mount Olympus. Small mounds of red sand were piled in the corners and in the wrought cracks of the rock walls. The two Dotok stopped in front of a door tall enough for a suit of armor. Caas matched the number on the door to a piece of paper in her hand.

"This is it," she said. "You ready?"

"I still don't understand this human ritual. We recited the oath of service when we joined the Home Guard. I don't know why we have to do…whatever is on the other side of that door. We fought the Ruhaald with Elias and Bodel. Aren't we Iron Hearts already?"

"We're Iron Hearts when they say we're Iron Hearts. The humans keep calling us 'slick sleeves' because we haven't been accepted into a team. This is what we have to do." Caas straightened her overalls and smoothed down her quills.

"I'm going first." She reached up to knock on the door but Ar'ri grabbed her sleeve.

"I'm bigger. I'm going first."

"I'm older and you lost the coin flip. Don't make me punch you before we go in there."

"Fine. Go." Ar'ri clicked his beak. "Mom and Dad would be proud. Couple low listers like us fighting in the best fighting unit the humans have."

Caas rapped her fist against the door three times. A metal slot slid aside, and a pair of blue eyes looked at her. One half of the man's face was slack, the effects of a stroke Bodel suffered years earlier on Takeni when he was removed from his armor after being badly wounded.

"Who goes there?"

"Caas Val Howsa of the Dotok—" The slot slammed shut.

"That's not what they told us to say." Ar'ri

24

shook his head.

"Shut up." Caas knocked again.

The slot opened again.

"I do not know," she said.

The door opened inward, just enough for Caas to step inside.

Suits of armor formed a cordon leading to a table covered in a thick burgundy cloth. Ten soldiers stood in front of the suits on either side, all humans wearing simple overalls with different patches on their shoulders. One suit of armor knelt on one knee next to the table, Elias.

Colonel Carius, the leader of the Armor Corps, stepped up behind the table and lifted a sword with a straight guard and rounded pommel emblazoned with an iron cross. He leveled the tip at Caas.

"Come forward!" Carius bellowed. The door shut behind them.

Bodel walked slowly, leaning heavily on a cane for support. They passed the second pair of soldiers when a woman with a scarred face stepped in front of Caas.

"This one is unworthy," she said. "I do not know her deeds."

"I am Caas—" A backhand slapped the Dotok across the face and staggered her back a step.

The soldier pointed a bloody hand, cut against Caas' beak, at Caas.

"No, you're not. I still do not know your deeds."

Caas' face stung, but she fought back anger.

"I fought the Xaros on Mars. I defended Phoenix from the drones. I fought beside the Iron Hearts against the aliens' commander. I spilled Ruhaald blood to save soldiers and doughboys under siege. I—"

"You?" A Hussar stepped away from his armor, a sword with a curved tip hanging from his belt. "All I see is weakness."

Caas was frozen, unsure how to respond. A nudge from Bodel sent her walking toward the next challenger.

"This is not a place for lies," he said. "I will see proof for myself, or you will pay a price."

Soldiers grabbed her by the arms and forced

her to her knees. She struggled briefly until Bodel's hand touched the base of her neck. The Hussar drew his sword with the hiss of metal on metal and set the blade against the other side of her neck. The blade was honed to a razor's edge and inches from her exposed flesh.

Bodel touched the back of her head and pushed her face toward the ground. She felt fingers against the neural-plugs in the base of her skull, where she connected to her armor, then the blade at her neck flicked away.

"She has given her body to the Corps," the Hussar said. "She may be worthy." The grasping hands released her and she continued toward Carius and Elias.

"Who is the petitioner?" the colonel asked Elias.

"She still does not know."

"Does she know why she fights?" Carius asked Caas.

"I was weak," Caas said, "just a child when the Xaros came to Takeni. My mother, my father, they died so that my brother and I could get away.

Marines saved us, but it was armor that protected us. We were worthless orphans but you saw us as...something worth protecting. Earth took us in, and we knew the Xaros would come back. I wanted to fight, to save my people, my new home. If I was going to fight, then I would wield the strongest weapon there is." She thrust a finger at Elias.

"Will you have her?" Carius asked Elias.

"I do not know who she is," Elias said.

"I am—" She caught herself when Bodel clenched his fist out of the corner of her eye. Several long seconds passed as Caas struggled with what to say next.

"Take her away," Carius shook his head.

Bodel grabbed her with surprising strength, and another soldier took her by the other arm and they led her away from the table.

"No! I'm not leaving like this." Caas struggled until the two soldiers pulled her off her feet and dragged her toward the entrance. "I know who I am—let me go! I am armor like you. I am armor!"

Caas fell to the ground.

"I heard something," Elias said. "Maybe she

does know."

She got up and stalked toward the table.

"I...am...armor!"

Applause broke out from the soldiers behind her. They stepped away from their suits and clustered around her, smiles across their once taciturn faces.

"Will you have her?" Carius asked Elias.

"She is an Iron Heart," Elias said.

Carius reached into a pocket and pulled out a small metal pin, a gray heart with two tiny brass spikes on the back.

"This belonged to another soldier," Carius said. "One who earned her place beneath Mount Olympus and at the right hand of God. Will you take it?"

"Kallen?" Caas asked.

Elias nodded his head.

"I will honor her memory and her deeds," Caas said.

Carius stepped around the table and pressed the pin just against the outer layer of her jumpsuit.

"Sir, what're you doing?"

Carius reached back, then slammed a punch

against the pin, knocking Caas against the soldiers around her and driving the spikes into her flesh. The pin embedded in her chest stung, and a trickle of blood stained her uniform, but Caas kept her composure.

"We have an Iron Heart!" Carius thrust his fists into the air.

Soldiers shook Caas' hands and offered words of encouragement that were lost in the overwhelming moment. She looked up at Elias, who turned his helm to the side slightly, and gave her a slow nod.

CHAPTER 4

Within the Crucible's command center, two artificial beings clustered around a holo tank. Stacey Ibarra pressed her hands against the tank's raised edge and leaned toward the re-creation of the Crucible floating before her. The gargantuan thorns comprising the wormhole gate moved slightly, like an urchin's spines against a gentle tide.

The Qa'Resh probe floated over the holo tank, its light an angry red.

"Are they done yet?" she asked.

Her grandfather, Marc Ibarra, present in the form of blue and white hologram, reached into the tank and made a quick gesture. The table zoomed to a slight gap in the circumference where a Xaros drone was attached to an unfinished thorn, held fast to the surface by long stalks. The drone's other stalks spun glowing thread from a cube of omnium into a basalt-colored material, layering it onto the gap a few feet at a time.

Floating over the drone was a man with no space suit, his knees and hands bent into a lotus position. In the light of the drone's work that smeared across his swirling surface, it was possible to see he had no face.

"We don't want them to finish," Ibarra said. "We're not ready. Not yet."

"Can they take a break at least?" Stacey tried to raise her hands from the tank but found them frozen against the railing. With the sound of cracking frost, she pulled them away and wiped rime from her forearms and shoulders, shivering against an imaginary cold.

Ibarra frowned and sent a quick command to the room's environmental controls to reduce the humidity down to nothing. The bone dry air would be uncomfortable for Shannon, waiting against the outer walls, but he'd send her away soon enough. Ibarra's body had died decades ago, but his consciousness remained within the Qa'Resh probe that once linked back to Bastion, the Alliance against the Xaros.

Stacey had returned from Bastion in a body not her own. The simulacrum bodies, as the Qa'Resh called them, were meant to keep Stacey ageless and safe from harm while at the Bastion space station. The Xaros' sudden attack on the heart of the resistance against their advance across the galaxy had called for a sudden evacuation—and for Stacey learning the truth of her situation.

Ibarra regretted keeping the truth hidden from his only granddaughter. He'd meant to reveal everything to her once she'd become comfortable with her position as Earth's ambassador to Bastion. He'd engineered her birth as something a bit more than human to serve as the permanent ambassador. Telling a woman in her early twenties that she'd never have the life she'd envisioned—marriage, children, aging—wasn't something he thought she could handle.

Damn me for thinking I was so clever and she so naïve, he thought.

In her simulacrum body, Stacey looked like a normal human at first glance. Her porcelain-smooth skin, emotionless eyes and neck-length hair that flexed as if made of heavy wire were unnatural compared to Shannon, the fifth re-creation of Ibarra's longtime associate, hitman and provocateur, standing behind her.

Stacey had spent years in her simulacrum body on Bastion without being aware of her altered state, but once she'd been taken away by the Qa'Resh during their retreat from the Xaros attack, a particular difference from her flesh-and-blood body had come to the fore. Her body was cold, like the kiss of artic wind against bare flesh. Stacey had refused to set foot on Earth since her return, confiding in Ibarra that she was terrified of being labeled as a freak or a monster.

Ibarra had promised her that a solution was available, one that he was about to deliver.

A line of text appeared next to Torni.

"The new material has to cure," Ibarra said. "Jimmy can divert his attention to you in a few minutes."

"Will Jimmy finally explain why I've had to

stay like this for days?"

Static washed over Ibarra's hologram.

"The Naroosha badly damaged the Crucible before the *Breitenfeld* and the Mars fleet blew them all out of space. The self-repair protocols barely kept this place from flying apart. Then you and the Qa'Resh popped up on Jupiter and told us the Xaros are using wormhole technology. That means they could be here, Earth, at the time of their choosing…unless Jimmy and our crystalline friends, the Qa'Resh, keep pumping a quantum distortion field through the Crucible to keep the enemy from opening a portal right over Phoenix."

"I spent years like this on Bastion." Stacey looked to her hands and flexed her fingers slowly. "The ignorance was bliss, but now I feel like my entire body is one big itch I can't scratch. I don't know how Torni does it."

"Your situation—unlike hers—has a solution. I have a spot of business to attend to first. Shannon?"

Shannon stepped away from the outer wall and came down the stairs leading to the holo tank at the bottom of the room's central recession. She wore a simple work jumpsuit over a thin space suit with an Ibarra Corporation patch on her left shoulder, the standard uniform of civilians assigned to spaceports and logistics efforts across the solar system.

During their many decades together, Ibarra had seen Shannon shift identities from a diplomat's faux-spouse to jailer to indigent within less than twenty-four hours. Her ability to slip into whatever role was needed—and her utterly ruthless nature—made her an asset he never wanted to lose. Just by glancing at the uniform she wore, Ibarra could guess most of what she was about to say.

"Public sentiment against the Ruhaald is still hostile, but not to a degree we can't manage," Shannon said. "Knowledge that three of their ships dropped inert nukes on cities is mostly contained."

"Mostly?" Ibarra asked.

"Everyone that had eyes on the nukes has been reassigned elsewhere in the system after a stern warning to keep their mouths shut about how crucial those Ruhaald 'devices' are to the war effort. We're monitoring them for compliance and all but one bought into the cover story of how we'll reverse engineer the technology. Hence the 'mostly.'"

Shannon swiped her fingers over a forearm screen then flicked her hand at the holo tank. The employee jacket of a balding man in his late forties popped up.

"James Howlett. Assigned to third munitions command," Shannon said. "Lost a couple friends on the *Stockholm* when the Naroosha destroyed it. Has a healthy hatred for the Ruhaald, guilt-by-association sort of thing. Mr. Howlett has pics of the nuke that landed outside Phoenix and sensor logs of the radiation coming off the warhead. The nuke inhibitor field that kept the bomb from going off also futzed with his data, so he's waiting to break the story until he can explain those errors."

"And he didn't take our standard 'keep quiet or else' spiel to heart?" Ibarra asked.

"He saw right through me. Swore he'd expose the whole conspiracy, yadda yadda, tinfoil hat, etcetera," she said.

"I hate it when the conspiracy theorists are right. We need the Ruhaald for what comes next. Why didn't you just liquidate him then and there?" Ibarra asked.

"Jesus, Grandpa," Stacey said, crossing her arms over her chest, "do you always murder people who get in the way of your plans?"

"Not always. Bribes. Gaslighting. Sudden real or manufactured revelations of deviant conduct. Killing is a last resort, but if Shannon's here, then the situation is more complicated than she's let on."

"Howlett has incriminating evidence squirrelled away online and hinted at a number of dead-man switches," Shannon said. "I need you to wipe it before I close his file."

"You mean murder him," Stacey said.

"My dear," Ibarra said as he clasped his hands behind his back and walked around the holo tank, "the Ruhaald fleet sits at void anchor many thousands of miles away from Earth. Macro cannons on Ceres and Luna are trained on them, ready to blow them into chum if they so much as move without our permission. We've got them at our mercy. It's bad enough that lives were lost both when they turned on us and during their little…biological incident with the doughboys. If the general public learns they tried to nuke us, the little people will start screaming for blood, trials, all manner of distractions that we don't need right now. So if I send Shannon to nip this problem in the bud, I won't lose any sleep."

"Why can't we resolve issues with a bit of openness? That man holds the truth. Why stifle it?" Stacy asked.

"High-minded ideas and honor work until they don't. Ask Caesar. You saw what happened on Bastion when the Vishrakath decided the rules needn't apply to them anymore." Ibarra nodded to Shannon. "Take care of him. Oh, and send the Dotok over when you see them in the shuttle bay."

The agent gave a half smile and left the room.

The Qa'Resh probe's surface shifted to ocean blue and it descended slowly. The holo display vanished as the probe came to a stop.

"The Crucible functions at 98.887% efficiency," the probe said. "The wormhole disruption field extends to the inner Oort cloud but will not go much farther, given the many uncharted comets and dense asteroids. I will remind you of my suggestion to better map the outer solar system four years, two months and eight day—"

"Yes, I remember." Ibarra waved a hand in the air. "You don't have to be right about everything."

"Is there a point to your bickering?" Stacey asked.

"Assuming the Xaros do not have a way to overcome the disruption field, the Crucible will be fully assembled and operational within three days," the probe said. "We will be able to access the entire Xaros gate network."

"If Malal's codex can deliver," Stacey said.

"He's already had some success. More on that later," Ibarra said. "Jimmy, are you ready?"

The probe floated toward a waist-high plinth in the center of the room. A ring of light broke around the base as the plinth rose into the air. Bright clouds of steam spat from the base, forming into a thin fog. A clear cylinder came up beneath the plinth. Ibarra made out a silhouette of a woman within the cylinder.

He walked through the fog and stopped a few steps from the tube containing his granddaughter's true body. Stacey's eyes were closed, her form perfectly still.

"What…" said the Stacey inside the simulacrum body from behind Ibarra. "What did you do to me?"

Ibarra turned around. Fog coalesced into snow and fell around the feet of Stacey's simulacrum. Her perfect doll face held firm as a sculpture. Even without seeing emotion on her face, Ibarra knew that his granddaughter was distraught.

"Stasis," Ibarra said. "Your flesh and blood remained here while your consciousness went through a conduit to Bastion where a simulacrum body waited."

"The quantum entanglements needed to transfer so much data are fragile and time-consuming to establish," the probe said. "Sending ambassadors to and from Bastion was the only viable solution the Qa'Resh had to coordinate the resistance to the Xaros."

Stacey leaned toward the cylinder, peering at herself.

"I'm in there…and I'm out here. Which one is the real me?"

"I'm not Confucius or Saint Augustine, Stacey. All I cared about was that it worked," Ibarra said.

"You cared about something?" Stacey's face snapped toward her grandfather. "If only you'd taken the time to ever care about me. You think I grew up wanting to be your damn science experiment? Sent off to God knows where to play politics with a bunch of aliens that saw us as nothing more than a means to an end? Get me out." Stacey thrust a finger at the probe. "Get me out of this thing right now so I can live my life like a human being."

"Stand still," the probe said. A tendril of light stabbed out of the probe and into the top of Stacey's head. Her spine straightened and her face tilted up.

"You have her?" Ibarra asked.

"The transfer won't take long. Her reactions don't conform to our models."

"That's because we were going to wait a few more years before telling her the truth. Give her time to *want* to be effectively immortal. Realize the importance of what she did for us on Bastion. Unfortunately, the enemy had a vote."

42

"Will she cooperate with the next phase? Her presence raises the probability of success significantly."

Ibarra gestured at the holo tank. Video feed of the *Breitenfeld*'s cargo bay came up. Rows of crew members were frozen in place, enthralled by Malal's stasis field that would keep them alive during the years it took for the ship's jump engines to recharge in deep space. Ibarra would have thought the video was paused, were it not for Stacey walking through the ranks. She stopped in front of Hale, his mouth open in mid-command, his hand pointed at Cortaro.

Stacey reached out and gently ran her fingers down the side of Hale's face.

"You will leverage her hormonal imbalance to gain her compliance?" the probe asked.

"She has a crush on him, a crush she doesn't know what to do with. Stacey was always shy around boys. Growing up surrounded by many armed and unfriendly bodyguards with specific instructions to dissuade any suitors didn't help her social skills." Ibarra dismissed the video.

"So I'll drop a few hints that Hale needs her.

She'll volunteer to go and then we'll cross our fingers. Tell me, Jimmy, am I going to hell?" Ibarra asked.

"Your concept of a positive or negative post-biological state has never been my concern," the probe said.

"The question might not even be valid. My body died decades ago. Maybe my soul is in the afterlife reaping what it sowed and this consciousness is all just an elaborate fake of the man it used to be."

"During our partnership you resisted such discussions, claiming they drove you to imbibe alcohol. Such an outcome is impossible in your current state," the probe said as the ribbon of light flowing to Stacey's head thinned.

Within the cylinder, Stacey's flesh-and-blood body awakened with a gasp. A panel slid down and Stacey stumbled out.

"I was...was in the white abyss again," she said. Her fingers pressed against her cheeks as her lips smacked over dry gums. "I'm thirsty. Hungry. Cramps. I never thought I'd be so happy to feel so miserable."

Stacey turned around and found herself face-to-face with the simulacrum body. She let out a brief scream and backed away.

"I'll have some food brought up," Ibarra said.

Stacey didn't respond. Instead she raised a hand and hesitantly reached toward the statuesque doppelgänger. There was a slight hiss as her finger touched her other forehead. Stacey yelped in pain and snapped her hand back.

"Why is it so cold?" she asked.

"The details of the simulacrum hosts are not available to me," the probe said. "Please step aside."

The Stacey's previous body place inside the cylinder and the dais sank back into the floor.

"Will you destroy that…thing…for me?" Stacey asked.

Ibarra glanced at the probe.

"Stacey," he said, "just because Bastion was destroyed doesn't mean the Alliance is gone forever. There's still a chance we could—"

"No. I'm a real girl now. No more strings on me."

Light rippled up and down the probe. "The simulacrum were built to withstand degradation.

Disposal is not a simple option."

"Toss it into the sun," Stacey said, shaking her head from side to side. "Use it as target practice. Open a wormhole into the center of God-knows-where and maybe some alien race of anthropomorphic hamsters will find it and worship it as a deity. I don't care. I never want to see it again. Understand?"

A door along the outer ring opened and a pair of doughboys pushed a cylinder identical to the one beneath the dais into the room on an anti-grav sled. Frost covered the cylinder's surface.

Ambassador Pa'lon followed the doughboys. His simulacrum self was tall, straight backed and wearing a white tunic over brown pants with loose, wide legs. He carried a walking cane of gnarled wood but didn't use it for support.

"Stacey...I believe this is the first time I've actually met the real you," Pa'lon said.

"Likewise," she said.

"Not quite." Pa'lon tapped the walking cane against the cylinder the doughboys had pushed down the wide steps and knocked a hunk of loose ice away.

Inside was the aged version of the Dotok ambassador. Patches of white mottled the skin and quills of the alien within.

"Your intended biological vessel is near the end of its usefulness," the probe said. "Given the tumors present in your lungs and failing lymphatic system, you have an eighty-nine percent chance of expiration within the next six months. Heroic measures increase the rate of survival to—"

"Cease your prattle." Pa'lon's thick "hair" furled in annoyance, knocking a tuft of snow loose from the ice-cold quills. "I know what this means."

"Pa'lon, the council of Firsts and the Dotok have stood beside us against the Xaros and the Naroosha treachery," Ibarra said, "but you and Stacey were the first to forge our partnership. We would hate to lose you to something so mundane as old age."

"The council already approves of the Qa'Resh plan to end the war...or lose it in a very slow and painful fashion. The Dotok populace on Hawaii and our space-borne military will need more convincing, and I can't do it in this...what did you call it, Stacey?"

"A golem," she said.

"We Dotok may be a spacefaring civilization, but we have our foibles," Pa'lon said. "We believe the soul and body to be in perfect unison until death. My bifurcated existence is the stuff of old stories told around the hearth to frighten children. Trying to convince any of my people looking like this would be the same as you going on TV with feathery wings and a hoop of light over your head."

"No, Pa'lon, the other one," Stacey said.

"Leather wings and horns? Red skins?"

"That's it."

"So confusing. My toddler grandchildren are terrified of me," Pa'lon said, raising his hands in front of his chest and squeezing his fingers together with a squeak of rubbing ice, "and I can't even hold them. I would rather die in bed surrounded by their fat, smiling faces than live forever like this."

"At least you two have options," Ibarra said with a snort.

"It will be a few more minutes before I can conduct the transfer. Your mind has significantly more information present than the younger Ibarra," the probe said.

48

"What's that supposed to mean?" Stacey asked.

"That I'm old and tempered with wisdom," Pa'lon said. "Convincing others of that is much easier when I look like a wizened sage. I never thought I'd be happy to return to this broken-down old thing." The Dotok ambassador wiped frost off the cylinder and leaned close to his flesh-and-blood body. His beak clicked twice.

"Ibarra," Pa'lon said as he stood up and turned to the hologram, "there is some concern among my people regarding the Qa'Resh plan. It deals with Malal. Is putting so much trust in him wise?"

"Like it or not," Ibarra said, "Malal has upheld his side of the bargain—can't say the same of our 'allies' on Bastion. We need him to finish construction on the Crucible and lead us to the Apex, where we can strike at the heart of the Xaros."

"We don't need him," Pa'lon said. "Torni can finish the Crucible. We have the codex Malal recovered from his vault hidden in the void between the stars. The Dotok concern deals with what comes next. Could you share why Malal is even helping us?"

"The Xaros can open wormholes to anywhere in the galaxy," Ibarra said. "If they aren't sending another invasion force here through their gate on Barnard's Star, then they could still jump in beyond our disruption bubble. Time is not on our side."

"You gave an answer, but not to the question I asked," Pa'lon said.

"I like you, Pa'lon, but you'd never make it as a human politician." Ibarra looked at Stacey and raised an eyebrow to her. Stacey knew the price of Malal's cooperation; she was the one that had negotiated the particulars with the ancient entity. Crossing her arms over her stomach, she looked away.

"You'll have to take that question up with the Qa'Resh," Ibarra said. "Everything's on a need-to-know basis with them, but all I need to know is that we've got a shot at ending this war before we all drown beneath a tidal wave of drones."

"So you want me to go back to my terrified people and tell them not to worry?" Pa'lon asked.

"Fear doesn't do any one of us any good right

now," Stacey said. "Malal only wants one thing—revenge. And we are not the target of his vendetta. Also, we have a device in his chest that will melt him down to subatomic goo if he steps out of line. So there's that."

"What did you say when the Xaros and the banshees charged toward Takeni?" Ibarra asked.

"I told them the mightiest ship in the galaxy, the *Breitenfeld*, was coming to save us. That humans were warriors without peer and singlehandedly beat the Xaros to save their own world," Pa'lon said. "I may have embellished a bit about how tall you were and he size of Captain Valdar's ship. No one has complained."

"Then 'embellish' some more," Ibarra said. "Success needs no explanation. Defeat allows none."

The probe blinked several times. "Please step closer. I am ready to begin."

Pa'lon set the walking cane against the cylinder holding his true body.

"One last time," the Dotok said as he gave the glass a quick tap.

CHAPTER 5

Shannon hurried down the stairs of the small shuttle cooling beneath an overcast sky. The Phoenix spaceport serviced 24/7 traffic coming into and out of the planet's de facto capital, but her landing pad was almost eerily silent. A steady stream of Mule and Destrier transports rumbled overhead, each flown by pilots that knew her tarmac was "no-go" terrain. When he was alive, Marc Ibarra cultivated an air of secrecy. The richest man in human history claimed— in public—that he valued privacy, while using his considerable influence—in private—to affect world events for decades on end. The reputation remained even after his consciousness took up residence in the

Qa'Resh probe, which suited Shannon's purposes quite nicely.

She strode toward a waiting ground car, the door already open and in-engine wheels humming with energy. The car came with an auto-driver that asked no questions and had its logs altered or erased after every trip. Anonymity and deniability had served Shannon well during her decades of service to Marc Ibarra. The same perks made her mission for her Naroosha masters even easier.

"Broadway and Gilbert," Shannon said as she sunk into the leather-bound seat. The door went opaque as it slid down and shut with a *thunk*. The car pulled ahead with a whine of electric motors.

This Shannon—a procedurally generated person molded off the memories and form of a long-dead woman named Shannon Martel—had awoken knowing exactly what she was and her true purpose. Previous iterations believed they were the original woman in every respect, but not this one. Why Ibarra decided to keep up that charade was of no concern to this Shannon. The Naroosha had brought her to life with a mission: deliver Earth and the proccie technology to her alien masters at any cost.

Serving as Ibarra's enforcer only made that mission easier. Her team of like-minded individuals, all from the same batch of proccies that came out of the crèche on the Crucible just after the Naroosha defeat, held positions across the solar system— positions of increasing importance as time went on— and Shannon provided an invisible hand to maneuver them through the solar system's military and nascent civilian government.

Her car zipped around traffic and breezed through intersections where the stoplights conveniently changed out of sequence to facilitate her passage. Bars of shadow swept over the cabin, cast by broken beams from the remains of a skyscraper. The Xaros attack had wrecked whole swaths of the city. With the populace safely underground, the defenders had little compulsion to prevent collateral damage. She shook her head at a collapsed munitions factory, the roof caved in like a spoiled soufflé. An armor soldier's rail-cannon shot had torn through the entire factory and ruined the delicate machinery inside.

Probably worth it, she thought, *most of the city*

survived.

Ibarra Corporation robots and work crews began reconstruction soon after the Ruhaald ships had retreated from the sky, sectioning off whole city blocks at a time. While she knew she was functionally invisible to the surveillance systems across the city, thanks to facial-recognition protocols that automatically erased signs of her passage, field-craft traits from decades of espionage still guided her. Shannon waved a hand across the windshield and brought up a map. She double-tapped a damaged building near her destination and rerouted the car to stop near a demolitions work crew.

The car slowed as it veered around massive hauler trucks waiting in a line that stretched from a two-story-high excavator. Shannon popped the door up and slipped out of the still-moving vehicle. She snatched a construction helmet off a coffee station behind the foreman's trailer and melded into the crew of workers and robots meandering around the collapsed remnants of a housing tower.

She changed her gait to match the exhausted men and women around her, becoming just another overworked person trying to function through the trauma suffered by their once fair city. Shannon caught sight of warning tape wrapped around exposed sections of rebar and a group of workers in bright-yellow coveralls. There was her target.

She walked along the hastily created perimeter of tape and saw a wrecked Condor bomber half-buried within the rubble, torpedoes still attached beneath the wings. Shannon's steps quickened. The damaged torpedoes had denethrite explosive warheads that could rip a ship apart and she didn't want to be around them any longer than necessary.

James Howlett, the man she'd told Ibarra was planning on exposing the Ruhaald attempted nuclear strike, stood in the center of a scrum of the yellow-clad explosive ordnance team. He was stocky and had several days' worth of stubble across his face. Holding up a data slate showing the crashed bomber and loose lines, Howlett outlined his plan for recovering the still deadly weapons from the wreckage. Shannon waited impatiently. Once he noticed her, Howlett gave her a slight nod.

"I want the mark-fours fit with full spectral

analysis kits before we send the robots down to get a closer look," Howlett said. "Mendoza, get with the site boss and have him shoot down any and all equipment larger than fifty tons right now. The warhead casings are cracked and that ups the risk of a vibration det. Go. Run like our lives depend on it."

A woman in yellow gave a hasty salute and took off running.

"The rest of you break out the robots and someone contact mortuary affairs. The tail gunner is still in there." Howlett clapped his hands twice and his team broke away. He sauntered over to Shannon.

"The hell do you want?" Howlett half-closed his left eye as he spoke, changing the meaning of his words to "welcome." Those procedurally generated humans born with the Naroosha imperative received a sublingual form of communication from their alien masters. The barest inflection, slightest shift in body language or facial tick combined with their spoken words changed the message to something only another Naroosha servant would understand.

To the uninitiated, the conversation between Howlett and Shannon was a run-of-the-mill work update. To each other, their words were far more sinister.

"The timetable has accelerated," Shannon said. "The Crucible is nearly repaired. Ibarra and the rest of the senior leaders will meet in the next few hours."

"Too soon," Howlett said. "Our faithful have coopted the crèches across the planet, not the entire system yet. The procedural-human generation rate is at full capacity to replace casualties from the Xaros invasion. Every human coming out of those tubes is loyal to our cause—even if they don't know it yet. Slow Ibarra's plans for a few more months and we can take the solar system in a bloodless coup once our numbers are enough."

"It does no good to seize the system if we can't deliver it—and the procedural technology—to the Naroosha," Shannon said. "We need the Crucible intact and a ship with a jump drive."

"The *Breitenfeld*...its crew is almost entirely true born. To infiltrate the ship will be difficult." Howlett pointed to the crashed bomber and rattled off statistics about defusing torpedoes. To cover his words.

"We don't need the crew," Shannon said. "Just the captain. Their senior staff meeting is our chance. I can kill the admirals, Valdar. Ibarra will replace them with procedurals. All loyal to us."

"And the Ruhaald fleet at high anchor?"

"I'll see that they're blamed for the attack. The Ruhaald won't be a problem for much longer."

Howlett narrowed his eyes at her. "How does this involve me?"

"I need explosives, enough to take out a room with a hundred people. Remote detonators…and no trail between us." Shannon removed a pen from her pocket and used it to sign a messy signature on Howlett's data slate. She let him keep the pen when she handed both objects back to him.

"Locker 97. Spaceport Terminal G," she said. "Drop the munitions off then take the poison before you leave the port. It will look like you were trying to flee the planet and chose death instead. The toxin is painless and quick."

"For the Naroosha," Howlett said.

"Your service will be remembered." Shannon

shifted out of the sublingual and scolded Howlett for the delay to the reconstruction efforts before she left.

****

Captain Valdar scrolled through an engineering report and frowned. The replacement battery stacks' efficiency ratings had gone down for the third day in a row. He typed out a terse text message to his chief engineer and pawed a hand over his desk, searching for a cold cup of coffee as he kept his eyes glues to the data slate.

The ventral rail gun batteries still wouldn't traverse a full 360 degrees. Valdar took a sip of the stale sludge that passed for coffee on his ship and contemplated just how big of a metaphorical stick he'd use to beat Utrecht before he got the battery fully mission-capable.

There was a knock at his ready-room door.

"Enter." Valdar didn't bother looking up as the door opened and shut with a hiss. His brow furrowed at a logistics report. A discrepancy on cargo weight from the *Breitenfeld* to Phoenix. Over a hundred kilograms of mass had somehow vanished while a Mule was in transit. One Private First Class Standish was on the manifest. This wasn't the first time he'd noticed Standish connected to such discrepancies.

A throat cleared.

Hale stood in front of the desk, his face turned away from Valdar.

"Ken? I-I didn't know you were back aboard." Valdar set the data slate aside.

"I'm a big boy now, Uncle Isaac," Hale said. "Amazing how many fires I have to stomp out as a company commander. I imagine it's worse for you and an entire ship."

Emotion welled up in Valdar's chest. Hale hadn't called him "uncle" since the Marine learned that his godfather had manipulated him during the Toth negotiations. Their relationship had been icy ever since.

"You want to sit down?" Valdar motioned to a chair covered by a fresh jumpsuit. "I've got..." he said, looking through his desk drawers and pulling out a pair of silver-wrapped ration bars, "nothing worth offering. Sorry."

Hale folded the jumpsuit over an armrest and sat. He bent forward, elbows resting on his knees.

"Did you hear what happened on Earth? Outside Phoenix?" Hale asked.

"Something about Ruhaald attacking an outpost. I had my own share of issues with them in orbit."

"I was on the Crucible when you brought the Mars fleet through the gate." Hale looked up and gave Valdar a half smile. "That was...satisfying to watch. The Naroosha didn't last long."

"They got a few hits in. They never answered our demands to surrender like the Ruhaald did and their ships didn't leave much for us to salvage like the Toth. Something tells me that's not why you're here, son."

"No." Hale shook his head. "In Phoenix, right after we killed the Xaros general and the Ruhaald parked themselves over our heads, I thought I'd found Jared." Hale recounted the rescue mission to the firebase outside Phoenix where he'd found a procedurally generated officer made to look and sound just like his absent brother. It took him a few tries to describe Lieutenant Bolin's fate.

"I...we never got to say good-bye to Jared," Ken said. "He joined the colony mission to Terra Nova while we were stuck out in the void. He told me he wanted to go accomplish something. I think all this—" he shook his head quickly, "attention I'm getting for the Toth and the war got to him."

"Now he's out there doing great things. Building a new home for humanity," Valdar said.

"And I'm the star of a movie I still haven't seen."

"Your father and I used to talk dad stuff all the time," Valdar said. "My boys were a bit younger than you two, but a lot of the same lessons applied. You know what your dad used to say about you two? That you were always competing against each other. Jared won a science fair and then you worked extra hard to win a diving trophy. You went for armor selection and Jared just had to be the honor graduate from his combat engineering course."

"Really? I never saw it like that."

"Parents know, Ken. We always know. Your

father let it go on—every dad wants to see his kids do well. He said at some point the two of you would realize you have to live your own lives, by your own terms. Jared finally decided it was his time."

"I just wanted to say good-bye," Hale said. "When I saw him lying there dead...not him...but I won't ever have that chance now. Mom and Dad are gone. Xaros took them. I can accept that. With Jared it just feels unfair."

Hale looked up, a tear running down his face. "You and Jared were all I have left from the old world. He's gone and then I pushed you away."

"No, son, that's my fault," Valdar said. "I put ideals before family. You know what? Someday this'll all end. I'll put the uniform away and then what will I have if I don't have you? I may have screwed up, but you're still my godson. Can you forgive me for that mess with the Toth?"

"You left my ass on Pluto."

"I was going to come back!" Valdar tossed his hands in the air. "Mars was screaming for help. Then Earth. Then the damn Ruhaald stabbed us in the back. By then you were already home."

Hale chuckled. "I saw all the equipment on the flight deck. Something big's coming, I can feel it. I'd rather we be on...good terms before it plays out. I forgive you for what happened with the Toth."

Valdar stood up and came around the desk. Hale stood up and the two shared a quick hug.

"We've got each other again," Valdar said. "I promise to keep it that way."

"Thanks, Uncle Isaac. Whatever comes next," Hale said, "we've got to win this thing. Nothing else matters if we lose."

CHAPTER 6

Shannon held a hand over her eyes to shield them from the too-strong sun bearing down on her. She shuffled forward with dozens of other men and women in a mishmash of uniforms and incomplete flight suits down a ramp from the Destrier that had brought them all to the Phoenix spaceport.

The smell of unwashed bodies came with a gust of wind. Specks of sand bounded across the tarmac as Shannon's hair whipped around her face.

The poor weather, for Phoenix, was a welcome relief from the holding cell aboard the Ruhaald ships. The aliens found her drifting in space, mere minutes of air remaining before asphyxiation would have ended her life. Her attempt to infiltrate another section of the Crucible with a trio of Marines had run into an unexpected problem when she'd missed her stop at the dome where the Crucible housed the omnium reactor.

She'd spent a long time in the void before being rescued, having decided not to activate her emergency beacons for fear of attracting the Ruhaald. How she ended up in space so close to the Crucible would beg a number of unfortunate questions, questions that would lead to the Marines she'd broken out of the alien's brig and the one Marine with the skills to reconnect the Crucible to the fleet locked down around the moon. That humanity seized control of the station and that Phoenix wasn't a radioactive hole in the ground told her that the mission succeeded without her.

Accepting death to ensure a mission, especially one so vital, hadn't bothered her. She'd spent her final hours contemplating what she'd seen in a procedural crèche and what it meant. There was another...her. Perfect down to the Caesarian section scars and long-healed bullet wounds. Part of her, the rational espionage agent, accepted that Ibarra wanted to keep an agent of her training and caliber at hand. Another part hated the holographic monster for such callous disdain. Having a replacement in the wings meant Ibarra had the option to discard her—any iteration of her—on a whim.

There, floating in the vacuum, as her space suit's life-support systems began failing, Shannon decided she wanted to live her own life. On her own terms. Then, the Ruhaald appeared and scooped her out of space.

The aliens hadn't interrogated her or demanded anything more than her name and if she required medical care. Given how different the amphibian species was from humans, Shannon was glad her needs stopped at a life-sustaining environment. What could a Ruhaald doctor do for her—besides open her up like a frog and marvel at her biology?

She'd spent days in a Ruhaald holding cell, alone. The smell of low tide and antiseptic still clung to her. She'd subsisted on damaged food packs that must have been pulled from a wrecked human warship and contemplated a new life away from

Ibarra. Then word came that she'd be repatriated to Earth.

"All freed prisoners of war please continue on to the debriefing room," said a captain standing on a small stage, her voice amplified through speakers. She pointed to a flag-draped doorway across the tarmac.

A group of civilians clustered around the doorway, clapping and smiling. They passed out cups of juice and small flags to the returnees as they passed. Shannon knew the old repatriation game; she'd gone through it several times over the course of her career. Beyond the doors would be a series of speeches from very concerned high-ranking officers and chaplains, promises of time off with family...then a DNA scan followed by a very collegial sit-down with an intelligence officer to identify any enemy sympathizers or collaborators among the freed POWs.

Shannon didn't have time for such pedestrian concerns, especially ones that could alert Ibarra to the fact that she was still alive.

She stepped through the doorway and into a hangar full of empty chairs and an even bigger stage.

Ibarra security robots formed a cordon to the seats, blocking off doorways and a hallway leading to a small enclosure within the hangar. She squeezed past a pair of haggard-looking Marines who had their eyes locked on a buxom woman clapping her hands on the stage and she went to a security robot, tilting her face up so the machine's optics could see her face.

Instead of gently escorting her back into line, the robot swung aside and let her pass. Every Ibarra security system came with overrides tuned to her biometric profile, something she'd take advantage of to slip away.

A door to a locker room opened at her touch and she darted inside. She waited a few seconds, listening for anyone that followed or took notice of her escape. After a minute, she found a locker with a set of clothes her size. Leaving the wire-mesh door slightly ajar, she went to the showers, stripping her space suit off along the way.

****

Shannon carried her tray of spaghetti and

meatballs to a table against a far wall of the spaceport's food court. Her instincts demanded she sit with her back to the wall and facing the entrance to keep track of anyone and everyone that decided this was the time for bland Italian fare.

Sniffing at her steaming plate, she felt her mouth water. The smell of under-seasoned tomato sauce was ambrosia compared to the days of nutrient paste. She sat down and gave the wad of money in a front pocket a reassuring pat. Cash came back in vogue after the great crash of '37 wiped out financial data across the planet; trust in debit cards and electronic fund transfer hadn't. She'd pickpocketed a half-dozen unsuspecting travelers in the spaceport and now had enough to live on for at least a week.

As she dipped a hunk of stale garlic bread into the red sauce and took a bite, she slipped a stolen Ubi from another pocket and pressed her palm against the screen. Lifting the occasional wallet would keep her fed, but staying in Phoenix for too long ran the risk of Ibarra learning she was still alive.

Her palm print overrode the device's security and it came to life, connecting to the local networks anonymously. The city's networks would automatically erase all trace of her passing. Working for Ibarra had its perks.

Shannon opened the personnel management dashboard for the city and glanced at a holo with departure times: shuttles to warships in orbit, transports bound for the outer planets, a science vessel bound for Sedna. With only a few edits to a file marked "recently deceased," she could take up a new life and go to any place in the solar system with a new identity. The path of destruction left by the Xaros threw the entire system into turmoil. No doubt there were plenty of people who'd been mistakenly listed as dead who were now trying to convince the personnel system that the rumors of their death were greatly exaggerated.

The thought of actual freedom kindled something in her heart that she hadn't felt for years...hope. She decided on Europa and found a dead computer technician whose skills would be needed.

A squat man walked into view just beyond the glass wall surrounding the restaurant. Judging by the way he walked, the small case in his right hand must have been heavy. He walked quickly, his gaze focused on a trash can in front of a Chinese fast-food kiosk. Shannon watched as he brushed past the can…and left a white slash against the rim with a piece of chalk.

Shannon's glimmer of hope turned into a shard of fear. The man with the case just made a dead-drop signal, a bit of spy craft centuries old. The man had something important to deliver and the mark meant he was certain he wasn't under surveillance. She knew…because that was a technique she'd used before with her contacts in Phoenix.

But I'm dead and I've never seen him before. Shannon pushed her tray away. *Why is he signaling me? I'm dead…but that thing I saw in the crèche…*

Shannon got to her feet and made for the exit. Her mind raced as she tried to grasp that the other Shannon was active and could be nearby ready to pick up the dead drop. What was it doing here? What did it want with that man?

She fell a few dozen yards behind the man with the case. He made a few attempts to spot anyone following, as well as halfhearted attempts to check his

Ubi while scanning around. Shannon maneuvered behind pedestrians and joined food lines every time the bagman stopped.

Amateur, she thought.

The man stopped at a locker and very gently placed the case inside.

Something heavy...but delicate? Shannon watched him retrace his steps to the place he made his original dead-drop mark. His hand swiped at the garbage can and left a right-angle line beneath the first. Drop in place.

Shannon looked at the departure board. The shuttle that would take her to Europa would begin boarding in a few minutes, but something about that dead drop set her instincts on fire. What did the other her want from this guy?

"I'm going to regret this." Shannon followed the man out of the terminal and into a concourse with a moving walkway leading to distant ground car and bus hub, lengthening her stride to catch up.

She gave the man's elbow a jog as she passed, signaling that she wanted him to follow her, then went straight for a maintenance door adjacent to the walkways. She saw him just behind her in the reflection off a glass panel next to the door. Her palm print against the handle overrode the locks and let her in.

She kept the door open and backed up as Howlett joined her in the dimly lit, and otherwise empty, hallway. Howlett looked confused and his cheeks flushed when the two finally came face-to-face.

"What locker did you use?" Shannon asked quickly. "You signaled the drop is down but it's not there."

"Nineteen," Howlett said. "Just like you said," his accent changing to American Southern. "All is as planned." He gave a nervous laugh and touched a pen fastened to a shoulder pocket.

"You were supposed to use fifteen." Shannon filled her words with annoyance. She'd berated her spies before and bluster would likely win against his weak demeanor. "Did you at least use the right lock combo?"

"Yes! One...thirty-seven...twelve." Howlett cocked his head to the side and said, "You're expected back on the Crucible." He added an odd inflection to the last word.

"You've already put too much exposure on us. Return—" Howlett snapped a jab into her throat.

Shannon stumbled back, croaking as she tried and failed to breathe, and dodged a hasty kick that pulled Howlett's balance forward. Shannon twisted her hips and smashed her shin against the man's knee. He fell forward, one hand grabbing her by the sleeve and bringing her down with him.

Her lungs burning, Shannon hammered a fist against Howlett's face. His nose broke with a crunch of cartilage. He jerked Shannon's arm aside and rolled on top of her, his strength and mass more than her lithe frame could fight. He pinned her to the ground with his bulk, blood pouring out of his nose and across her face.

She heard the click of a pen.

Howlett reared up, the pen grasped in his fist like a dagger. He grunted and swung it down, bending at the waist.

Shannon got an arm up and struck her forearm against his, deflecting the strike aside. With

76

one hand, Shannon grabbed him by the shirt and jerked him close. With her other hand, she cocked her thumb out and stabbed it into his eye.

Howlett wailed in pain and rolled off her, a palm pressed against his ruined eye.

Shannon wiped his blood away and finally managed a shallow breath. She looked around for anything to use as a weapon, but the hallway was empty. Turning her attention back to Howlett, she readied a stomp that would crush his skull…but he lay on his side, his body jerking in seizure.

The pen stuck out from his stomach, the tip embedded in his flesh. Howlett's eyes rolled into the back of his skull as white foam seeped from his mouth and mangled nose.

Poison, one she'd used before by the looks of what it was doing to Howlett.

She gave the dying man a quick pat down, searching for anything that might help her understand his purpose. He had nothing but his ID tag from a munitions unit. She touched her throat gingerly. She'd have a hell of a bruise in a few minutes, but she could breathe. She looked over her clothes. A little of his blood stained the dark-colored cloth, not enough to draw attention in passing.

"What the hell is going on here?" He'd known her. Answered her questions. A habit of flying into a homicidal rage wasn't a trait she wanted in her sources.

The drop.

Composing herself, she left the body behind and went back to the food court, her appearance attracting only a few glances from others. Locker 97 opened with the combination Howlett gave her...but it was empty. Shannon's head snapped around, looking for her doppelgänger. She caught a glimpse of a woman with a familiar walk just before she turned a corner.

"God damn it." She shut the locker and caught a peculiar order. Leaning closer, she took a deep sniff. Cordite and a faint scent of bleach. It smelled of a certain explosive she'd used many times before—denethrite.

A cold pit formed in her stomach. This wasn't how she and Ibarra worked. Something was very wrong with the entire situation. As much as she hated

Marc Ibarra at that moment, she still felt a degree of loyalty to his cause. Freedom could wait.

She took out her Ubi and tapped in a call to an emergency line to the Crucible…and got an error message. She tried two more backup channels and got the same result. The other Shannon must have changed the communications protocols.

If I go to the military or security services, she'll know, Shannon thought. *If she gets wind of something odd, she'll accelerate her plan. That's what I would do.*

"Flight Bravo Two-Zero now boarding for Ceres at Gate 12," came over the PA system.

Ceres. It wouldn't take much to redirect the flight to the orbiting Crucible.

Shannon ran for the gate.

****

The Crucible's air was cold and dry, which played hell with Shannon's sinuses as she walked down the hallway that curved around an auditorium. In a few hours, the admirals, generals and senior leaders from across the solar system would gather to discuss the next steps to defend the Earth.

There were no guards, but what did the unified commanders have to fear from each other? Ibarra's paranoia made sure that security fell to his most trusted aide.

Shannon keyed a command onto a forearm screen, disabling the cameras throughout the sector. She took a length of burn cord from a pouch and fastened it to the wall of the auditorium. The wire burned white-hot and cut out a lump of basalt the size of her head. It fell to the ground and disintegrated into pale embers.

A denethrite charge went into the hole and the Crucible's self-repair systems reformed the wall around the explosive, hiding it perfectly. A simple, low-frequency radio pulse was all Shannon needed to detonate the device.

She emplaced the next four charges around the outside of the auditorium. It would take only two of the explosives to kill everyone in the room, but she found no harm in adding a little extra as insurance.

Once humanity's senior leaders were dead, she'd manufacture evidence that the Ruhaald—still waiting their fate and under threat from macro-cannons—were responsible for the attack. The official inquiry would deduce that the aliens must have left sabotage devices behind when they surrendered the Crucible. The public would practically demand the Ruhaald be blown out of space. Once the new leaders came out of the crèche, there would be no one to oppose the Naroosha's takeover of the system.

Shannon ran her hand over the wall where the final device waited, unable to find a flaw in the repairs. She reactivated the communications and surveillance systems with a tap to her screen.

"—*annon!*" Ibarra screamed in her earpiece.

"Yes?" Shannon's face contorted in annoyance. Ibarra had become even more of an incessant pest since he became a hologram. At least he used to sleep back when he was alive.

"What the hell's going on over there in node four? Station command and I've been trying to reach you for almost five minutes."

"Either the Ruhaald or the Naroosha ripped out every surveillance system we had when they took the place over. Whoever reinstalled the cameras did a piss-poor job. The data lines are a rat's nest and the audio wasn't coming through. It took me a half hour to unscrew the problem. You're welcome."

"Fine. Give yourself a pat on the back. Make it two. Then get back over here. A shuttle en route to Ceres is losing life support and they've got to make an emergency landing. Come dissuade anyone from taking a look around. They might touch something delicate and you know how I hate it when strangers play with my toys."

Shannon sighed in relief. He bought her excuse.

"Moving," she said with a roll of her eyes. She couldn't wait until the Naroosha deleted him.

****

Ibarra paced around the dais, glancing up at the probe floating high above. Tiny lightning bolts of activity flit over its glowing surface. He passed by the cylinder holding Pa'lon's simulacrum body, which was covered by a black curtain.

"Why do you insist on pacing?" Stacey asked. She lifted a slice of pizza covered with pepperoni and onions out of a box and took a bite. "The food out of the omnium reactor tastes so much better than the crap from the fabricators. This is amazing."

"Glad you decided to use that precious resource to make yourself lunch," Ibarra said.

"There was a break between aegis armor production batches. I regret nothing." She took another bite. "Is there Molson beer in the reactor's database? Why didn't I think of that earlier?"

"Are you flaunting your ability to eat and drink just to piss me off? Because it's working."

"This could be my last real meal before we jump off to Ruhaald Prime. Then it's nothing but crap galley food for who knows how long. Don't spoil this for me," she said.

"Quantum connection established," came from the probe.

"'Bout time." Ibarra stopped pacing and faced the dais.

A small projection of a many-limbed Qa'Resh materialized in front of the Ibarras. Crystalline plates glinted over the being's dome-shaped upper body. An image of a middle-aged woman, her long hair in a braid over a shoulder, appeared in front of the Qa'Resh.

"We have a consensus with the Ruhaald queen aboard the *Forever Tide*," the woman said.

"At least something's easy," Ibarra said.

"Can she sway the other queens?" Stacey asked.

"Other queens? What other queens?" Ibarra whirled toward his granddaughter, his body alive with static.

"The Ruhaald aren't a unified whole like we are," Stacey said. "Their royalty work together as a synod, which barely makes sense to me, but I can slap the 'I believe' button for the negotiations. For what we're asking, the entire council will have to agree to our proposal."

"If you would accompany the expedition," Ibarra said to the Qa'Resh, "it would be a big help."

"Don't think I can do it?" Stacey asked, her nose rising in the air.

"Of course you can, my dear, but the more

the merrier. Same as any fight."

"Our lesser selves cannot survive away from the whole," the Qa'Resh said. "If Qa'Resh'Ta leaves, Earth will be vulnerable without us to maintain the quantum disruption field that prevents the Xaros from opening a wormhole above your skies."

"Didn't hurt to ask," Ibarra said. "We're nearly ready for the council. I'll brief Admiral Garret as to the particulars soon as he arrives. There was a small security issue that's being taken care of which reminds me that—"

A door along the outer wall opened and Shannon came down the stairs. She gave Ibarra and Stacey a smile.

"Speak of the devil," Ibarra said. "We need every last doughboy sequestered when Jarilla arrives. We don't want another incident so late in the game."

A door on the other side of the command center opened...and another Shannon stood in the doorway.

Ibarra looked at the Shannon standing next to him, then back at the other woman who was now racing down the stairs.

"What the hell?"

The Shannon next to him reached behind her back and drew a snub-nosed pistol, leveling it at Ibarra's chest and firing twice. Ibarra recoiled out of sheer instinct, his hologram unaffected by the bullets.

"Grandpa?"

Ibarra turned around and found Stacey leaning against the dais, an arm pressed against a bloody stomach.

"Stacey!" He reached for her as she collapsed to her knees, a dark line of blood escaping her lips and dribbling down her chest. Ibarra tried to grab her, but his projection lacked all substance.

Stacey let out a low moan and fell forward.

More gunshots snapped in the air. There was a cry of pain and the gun went skidding past Stacey.

"Stacey, you've got to get up! I can't help you like this," Ibarra said.

A pool of blood spread out from Stacey as her breathing slowed.

The two Shannons grappled against a control station, both sets of eyes alive with hate.

Ibarra tried to set his palm against Stacey's

head.

"You've got to get up, honey. Please, sweetheart, I need you to—"

Ibarra's hologram vanished.

One of the Shannons wrenched the other's head aside and smashed a hook into the other's jaw. Her knees buckled and she fell against the cylinder holding Pa'lon's body.

The other pinned an arm against broken ribs and spat at the doppelgänger.

"You're not Shannon Martel," she said, "and I should have killed you when I had the chance."

The other pushed herself to her feet and wiped blood from split lips.

"You're not little Eddie's mother," she said. "But deep down you know you're still the reason he and his father are dead!"

The woman jumped onto the other, banging her head against the cylinder and pulling the drape free. It fell over the two as they thrashed in a mass of flailing limbs and angry curses.

Pa'lon's simulacrum twitched. Its arm shot up and cracked the glass with a snap. The hand flopped against the casing like it was made of rubber before finally shoving the lid up on its hinge.

Marc Ibarra rolled himself onto the ground. The new body was all wrong, the limbs too long. The splayed feet didn't grip the floor and the fingers with one knuckle too many refused to move the way he demanded.

He tried calling to Stacey, but only gibberish came out from the beak of his mouth. Clawing his way to Stacey, he reached over her, picked up Shannon's gun and put a thick fingertip against the trigger. He rolled over and aimed the pistol at the melee.

The gun fired once and one of the Shannons reared back with a cry. The other woman looked at the Dotok body and raised a hand to stop him.

Ibarra shot her in the face. Both women lay still.

"Gogi!" Ibarra said. He worked his beak several times, trying to speak with another's lips and tongue. "Gogi ti raggathi."

"I cannot understand you," the probe said. The dais rose out of the ground, Stacey's blood streaking the side.

"One bullet caused severe lacerations to Stacey's heart," the probe said. "The other damaged her diaphragm and is currently lodged in her spine beneath the T10 vertebrae. She will expire in the next three minutes unless she receives immediate medical attention."

"Gogi ti raggathi!" Ibarra touched Stacey on the shoulder, instantly freezing the blood creeping up her clothing. He yanked his hand away.

The dais stopped and the casing slid aside. Stacey's simulacrum stepped out.

"Place her in the stasis chamber," the probe said.

Ibarra looked at the other body, the body Stacey hated so much, and hesitated.

"She will die if you do not."

Ibarra grabbed Stacey beneath her shoulders and dragged her into the chamber. Her blood spilled across his hands and arms, hardening into icy scabs within seconds. Her eyes fluttered for a moment. Just before the door slammed shut, she reached toward Ibarra and then she froze, drops of blood from her fingertips hanging in midair.

Ibarra's feet slipped on the bloody floor. He
pressed his face against the casing and slapped a palm
against the glass.

""Tacey!"

"I've begun the transfer, but the system was
not designed to work while the mind is under such
trauma. There may be some adverse long-term
effects."

Ibarra felt pins and needles along his hand.
The fingers shortened as the feeling spread across his
entire body. The pins became white-hot with pain as
they reached his face and neck. Ibarra pressed his
hands to his face and let off a yell that undulated in
pitch. When the pain subsided, he took his hands
away and saw a familiar reflection in the glass.

"Jimmy? What happened?"

"The simulacrum shells adopt their user's
neural pathways. The benefit should be apparent.
One of the procedural humans conforming to
Shannon Martel is still alive. Please investigate before
she interferes with Stacey's transfer."

Ibarra grabbed the gun from the floor and

stumbled toward the two women. Although he had a new body, after years of living as a hologram, walking proved a difficult task.

The Shannon he'd hit in the head hadn't moved. The other sat up against a workstation, her skin deathly pale and blood flowing from an exit wound beneath her clavicle.

"Hey boss," she said, "you're...here again." Her words came out slurred, a sure sign of shock from blood loss.

Ibarra aimed the pistol at her head.

"She's got denethrite. Don't know what for," Shannon said. She smacked her lips over a dry mouth. "Sorry I didn't come back. Just wanted to be free...for once."

"What denethrite?" Ibarra lowered the gun. "Where?"

"You tell Eric I'm sorry. Sorry for bringing him into this kind of life. Boss...let me go. I want to be with my little Eddie...and Tom." She looked up at Ibarra, her eyes struggling to focus. "Let me go. Please let me go."

Her head tilted backwards. Her breathing

stopped a moment later.

"Jimmy, I think there's a bomb somewhere on the Crucible. Find it."

"My available cognition is focused on saving Stacey and maintaining the field that keeps the Xaros out of our solar system. You have hands. Use them."

"Right. Forgot." Ibarra went to a workstation and swiped his hands through the holo field. He accessed systems slowly; he was used to simply willing the information to himself while he was part and parcel of the Qa'Resh probe.

Ibarra looked to his granddaughter, caught so close to death within the stasis chamber. A wavering ribbon of energy connected the probe to the ice-cold simulacrum standing nearby.

"Focus, Marc, focus," Ibarra said to himself as he scanned through station logs, flicking reports up around the holo field. "Jimmy, we made sure Shannon's personality matrix was utterly loyal to me and Stacey. What…one of them just did should've been impossible. The other kept to her conditioning."

"Your reasoning is sound," the probe said. "I am unable to assist with a deeper analysis during the transfer."

Ibarra swiped his hands through the holo field and tapped the icon for the procedural-generation crèche aboard the Crucible. Data scrolled through the field.

"The last Shannon to come off the line had her behavior conditioning altered...just before we took the station back from the Naroosha." Ibarra highlighted segments of text and opened a new search query. Profiles popped out of the Crucible's crèche file, each with red bands of text within their procedural-generation report.

"They've all been altered," Ibarra said. The holo field filled with an avalanche of profiles as they spawned from the crèche. "Every single proccie out of those tubes is compromised." Ibarra stepped away from the holo field, his hands balled in fists against his waist.

"Examine the other crèches," the probe said.

Ibarra stepped forward and pulled up the fifty different procedural-generation facilities across the planet. "No...," he said, "can't be..."

Compromised profiles by the tens of

thousands came up. Ibarra accessed the data from Mars and the outlying planets; that data returned clean.

"She's been busy," Ibarra said. "We worked hard, Jimmy, so hard to convince everyone that the proccies were safe. That something like this could never happen. Now we've got an insurrection just waiting in the wings."

"The transfer is nearly complete. Do you have a suggestion to deal with those compromised by the Naroosha?"

"They're a cancer. We must cut them out before they infect and destroy everything," Ibarra said.

Stacey's simulacrum let out a gasp. Her hand shot up, mirroring the gesture of the body frozen in the stasis chamber.

"Grand—" Stacey pulled her hand close to her face, looking over the frost along the gray metal of her fingers. Her head snapped to the stasis chamber. "No...I can't stay like this."

Ibarra closed the holo with a flick of a wrist and went to her. He put his hands over her shoulders

94

and she recoiled slightly.

"Wait, how're you…you stole Pa'lon's body?"

"You were dying. Options were limited. It's not like he wants it back."

"Your body is seconds from death," the probe said. "Its condition remains stable so long as it remains in stasis."

"You mean I'm trapped like this?" she asked.

"I'll get you out of there, Stacey. I promise. But right now we've got a serious problem to deal with." Ibarra went back to the workstation.

"Why the hell are there two Aunt Shannons? Why did one shoot me?" Stacey grabbed the curtain off the floor and draped it over the dead women. "There aren't any more, are there?"

"Stacey," Ibarra said, "this day is going to get a lot worse before it gets better. We have to find a bomb and then you need to get to Admiral Garret's conference before you lose any and all plausible deniability for what's going to come next."

CHAPTER 7

The Engineer existed within the Crucible network, his consciousness spread across the thousands upon thousands of gates connecting the many stars with habitable worlds and locations of archeological interest within Xaros-controlled space. He adjusted the quantum space between the gates, compensating for gravity tides and stellar events straining the connections.

The gates could compensate for the discrepancies on their own, but the Engineer took pleasure in perfecting his work. He sent an update for the entire network, increasing the overall efficiency by several tenths of a percentage.

He extricated himself from the network and was about to leave the Crucible in the system with the much larger and single-purpose gate connecting to the Apex...and felt something out of place in his near-perfect creation. A subtle fluctuation traveled through the network seemingly at random, a fluctuation resonating with the quantum state of omnium.

Rage coursed through the Engineer. That another being could meddle in his sanctuary appalled him to the core. He readied an energy pulse that would burn out the offending message...then hesitated. Who, aside from Xaros, could trespass here? The Engineer sent out his own fluctuation, an inverse wave that cancelled out the anomaly, answering the signal with his own.

A new fluctuation appeared, this one in the language of a long-dead civilization. A ripple of excitement coursed through the Crucible network as the Engineer responded to Malal.

****

Hale squeezed past a huddle of naval officers to the back of the auditorium aboard the *Constantine*. His shuttle had been en route to the Crucible for this briefing when the location was changed due to "scheduling conflicts"—according to the announcement that directed them to Admiral Garret's flag ship.

How someone could screw up when and where to have a meeting with the senior-most members of the military and other leadership figures nagged at Hale, but at least he knew where he—a junior Marine captain—was supposed to sit: as far toward the back of the room as possible.

Steuben towered over a section of mostly vacant seats in the back two rows and gave Hale a slight nod as he arrived. Lieutenants Jacobs, Bronx, Matthias and First Sergeant Cortaro rose to their feet when they saw Hale.

"Sir, you have some idea what's in store for us?" Jacobs asked. "I thought we'd overhear something but everyone's too scared of the XO to come close."

"You asked me to secure seats," Steuben said.

98

"One ship's officer asked me for a 'selfie.' I ate her data slate. No one has approached our position since then."

"He did," Cortaro said. "I don't think he even chewed it."

"Steuben, do I really have to ask you not to eat things like that?" Hale pressed fingers against his temples as a headache formed.

"You will note the many available seats," Steuben said.

"Any word why we had to come to the *Constantine*?" Bronx asked. "I kind of wanted to see the Crucible while not being shot at."

"None. I want you all to listen for the implied tasks of this mission. We have to do a HOLO jump then be thinking about..." A shiver passed through Hale as the air temperature suddenly plummeted. His breath formed into fog.

"Ken?" came from behind.

He turned and found Stacey Ibarra and a Ranger with an opaque facemask standing behind her. Stacey wore a standard void-ship uniform, coveralls and a thin vac suit bereft of markings, but her pale gray skin and still eyes made Hale uneasy.

"Stacey? I'm not surprised you've got a part in this," Hale said. He took a hesitant half step backward.

"Yeah, this…" she said, touching her porcelain-smooth skin, "this is kind of how the others know me. I'll be back to normal. Soon. Hopefully. I just wanted to thank you in advance for coming along. I know diplomatic missions aren't really your thing."

"Wait…why am I going on a diplomatic mission?" Hale asked.

"Is it the Toth?" Steuben let out a panther-like growl.

"No, not them." She glanced at the Ranger behind her.

"Who's this?" Hale asked.

"Oh, my new…new bodyguard! Grandfather insisted. This is C-Cletus. Yes, Cletus."

A murmur spread through the conference room as a pair of armed Marines stepped into the room. A tall Ruhaald followed and adrenaline dumped into Hale's bloodstream. The markings on the alien's armor depicted an unknown solar system carved into the chest plate. It wasn't a match for the armor of the Ruhaald that had killed so many doughboys in the desert outside Phoenix, one by the name of Tuk.

If Tuk had walked through the door, Hale would have taken a weapon from one of the guards and shot that alien in the head. Tuk had led an extermination against the bio-constructs to satisfy some sort of blood debt, killing many Marines as well as doughboys in the process. Hale's insistence that the Ruhaald be held responsible for war crimes had fallen on deaf ears.

"There's Septon Jarilla," Stacey said. "We're about to start. I'll see you…soon." She reached out and tapped Hale on the arm, her touch bringing a bite of cold with it. She and Cletus made their way to the front of the auditorium.

"Hale, there was something wrong with the Ranger," Steuben said. "He had no scent. Neither did she."

Hale rubbed his arm and sat down.

"Somehow I doubt that's the last oddity we'll

encounter today."

****

Stacey kept her back to the wall just off to the stand of flags near the front of the auditorium. The political entities represented by the flags no longer existed, but the sailors aboard the *Constantine*—and every other ship—clung to tradition. She could have sat in one of the front-row seats with the rest of the senior staff officers, but her body's cold aura had a noticeable effect on those around her. Her first attempt at a suit meant to insulate against the temperature difference had failed miserably.

Now she stood in front of nearly a hundred people, their eyes darting between her and the Ruhaald officer on the other side of the room. The mood was upbeat, almost excited. She understood: surviving the Xaros attack and wresting control of Earth back from traitorous hands deserved a celebration. Too bad their joy would be short-lived.

Did they know what she was? What kind of rumors would spread after enough people got a look at the perfect doll she'd become? She'd grown up the only heir of the richest man in human history. The nagging suspicion that people never looked at *her*, only at the mountain of baggage that came with her lineage, had plagued her since childhood.

Now…

"Look at them," her bodyguard said through her earpiece. "So full of hope. I almost regret bursting their bubble."

Stacey swiped a thumb over the throat mic on her suit to open a channel to the black-clad soldier and spoke softly. "We don't have a choice. Do we? Wait…I thought Jimmy was going to give the bad news."

"It'll be me, as far as they know," Ibarra said. "All the blame will fall on ghost me, which is fine. I've been a scapegoat since the fleet returned to Earth and found the place scoured clean of nearly every trace of human existence. Just keep up the ruse that I'm your bodyguard for a bit longer. If folks realize I've actually got an ass to kick, I might find myself thrown out of the nearest air lock. And 'Cletus'? Really?"

"I panicked. Shut up."

The room snapped to attention as Admiral Garret entered. The man looked like he'd aged a decade in the past weeks. The stress of coordinating an entire solar system against the Xaros attack while overdosing on stimulants had finally broken the man. A few days of forced bed rest and a regimen of nervous-system depressants had brought him back to normal. Whether his pride had recovered from the fact that Captain Valdar led the effort that saved Earth from the Ruhaald and Naroosha remained to be seen.

"Be seated." Garret took a stylus off his sleeve and stretched it into a pointer. "First, I must thank you all for your heroic efforts. We have survived because of you. The same Xaros that murdered billions have been beaten by us not once, but twice. Lives were lost. Ships destroyed, but the human spirit endured. As much as I'd like for us to take a well-deserved rest and appreciate the victory…we don't have that luxury."

A chill fell over the room as the implication of Garret's last words hit home. The lights darkened and a holo projector came to life.

"Here we go," Ibarra said.

"You worried?" she asked.

"You barely know Jimmy. Think after a few decades of working together he can't do a good impersonation?"

"You don't sound convinced."

"You barely know Jimmy."

A hologram of Marc Ibarra appeared behind a podium. A scale model of the solar system stretching out to the Kuiper Belt and Oort cloud came up next to him.

"Ladies and gentlemen, in the past hours the Crucible detected a number of quantum events out beyond the heliopause," the hologram said. Six ruby-red points appeared along the ecliptic solar system's plane. "The energy signature is consistent with wormhole gates. Telescopes captured these images."

Screens popped up over the hologram's head, each showing a white plane of energy over the backdrop of deep space. Tiny black specks flooded out of the wormholes, Xaros drones coming through by the tens of thousands each second.

Stacey watched as the once-confident faces of those assembled fell to reveal fear, or shifted into the expressionless mask of command used to hide any and all emotion.

"The drones arrive with very little velocity," the Ibarra hologram said. "Given their documented acceleration rates, I estimate it will take forty-nine weeks before the drones breach Pluto's orbit. Earth, days after that."

"Can we shut down the gates?" came from the audience.

"If I alter the Crucible's disruption field, it will leave us vulnerable to a closer incursion," the hologram said. "We cannot stop the Xaros from here. We can slow them down with graviton mines…those are already factored into the timeline."

"They'll never stop," Captain Valdar said from the first row. "The Xaros will flood the system unless we find a way to cut them off at the source."

"You tell him to say that?" Ibarra asked Stacey.

"Not everything is theater. Shut up," she hissed at him.

"That is our current assessment," the hologram said. Murmurs spread through the crowd.

Garret rapped his pointer against the side of the podium and the room fell silent.

"We are here for two reasons," Garret said loudly. "The first is to prepare for the evacuation of the solar system."

Stacey expected an uproar of defiance, outrage. The room stayed dead silent.

"We cannot defeat an enemy without number," Garret said. "Even with the procedural-generation facilities and automated fleet yards running at full capacity, the Xaros will either bleed us white through attrition or bury us beneath a flood of drones. We must save what we can."

Garret began outlining changes to ship construction and screening criteria for those who would—and would not—be selected for the outbound fleet.

"It doesn't matter," Stacey said to Ibarra. "The Xaros can open a wormhole to anywhere in the galaxy they want. We can run but we can't hide."

"Torni says the Xaros are reluctant to use

wormholes outside their Crucible network," Ibarra said. "They destroyed their home when a wormhole created a quantum fissure that annihilated all the matter in their galaxy. For them to take the risk of attacking Bastion and now here…it means they're desperate."

"So are we." Stacey squared her shoulders and cleared her throat as Garret gave her a quick glance. "Wish me luck."

"More details will come out as available," Garret said to his stunned audience, "but tell your command that there is hope. The second reason for this conference is to lay out a plan that can end this war once and for all. Ms. Ibarra?"

Stacey went to the podium and grabbed the side with both hands. She hoped the darkened room would hide the truth of her appearance as she tapped a small screen on the podium.

A map of the galaxy appeared next to her. Thousands of tiny red dots filled four-fifths of the star field; the remaining slice held the portion of the galaxy that the Xaros had yet to conquer.

"What you see are the known Crucible gates

across the galaxy," she said. "Only one is under our control, and once it is complete, it can tap into the entire network. Malal, a...technical expert, has managed to tap into the network and detected command directives that came through the noise of normal drone operations. The drones within star systems that have a Crucible send an enormous amount of data to each other and—through a light-speed-based broadcast system—to the maniples moving through free space. It's all automated and—"

Garret cleared his throat.

"Yes, my point. Here are the command directives." A jagged line bounced from a Crucible just at the edge of occupied space back to the far end of the galaxy. Another line began several hundred light-years from the first and traced back to the same star where the first message ended. A dozen more lines appeared, all taking different paths across the galaxy but either beginning or terminating in the same place.

Stacey flicked her fingers in the star field and the image zoomed in on a red dot on the very edge of the galaxy.

"This is Sletari, the first world to fall to the Xaros many thousands of years ago," she said. "This is the first Crucible gate they ever created, a place known as the Apex."

The galaxy shrank and a pulsing red dot appeared within the void beyond the Milky Way galaxy.

"While Sergeant Torni was a prisoner of war, she learned of the Apex's existence and that it houses nearly the entirety of the Xaros leadership. Most are in stasis. One of their leader caste was destroyed on Earth. At least one more is active and directing the war against us." Stacey shoulders drooped. "As for what the Apex is…"

The holo zoomed in on the pulsing red dot and a many-sided polyhedron made of pearlescent crystal came into view. A yellow dot a mere fraction of the size appeared next to it. A label next to the dot read THE SUN.

"It is a Dyson sphere," she said. "The circumference roughly equal to the orbit of Saturn."

Someone rose in the auditorium and shouted, "How the hell are we supposed to fight that?"

"At ease!" Garret thrust his pointer at the speaker.

"Destroying something of this size is difficult, I admit," Stacey said. "Also difficult is getting to the Apex, as Malal tells us we can't actually reach intergalactic space from our Crucible once it connects to the network."

Grumbling came from the audience.

"I said 'difficult,'" Stacey said, raising a finger in the air, "not impossible. Don't wet the bed just yet." A few chuckles helped her confidence.

"Once our Crucible is complete and it gains full access to the Xaros network, we can send a fleet to Sletari, seize control of the gate there and then launch an attack on the Apex." She flicked her fingers in the holo and it zoomed in on Sletari. A hazy outline of a Crucible gate appeared, but this one had multiple rings of thorns radiating away from its center.

"The Qa'Resh captured this image some time ago," she said. "Wormhole travel to and from deep space is an order of magnitude more difficult than what we've experienced. We believe this is why so few of the Xaros leadership caste operate within the galaxy. Only a few of their photonic-based life forms can translate back and forth to the Apex at any one time. But once we have control of this Crucible, code named Key Hole, we can send the Apex a special delivery."

The holo shifted to a wire diagram of an arcane device.

Captain Valdar let out a curse.

"This is a jump engine," Stacey said. "It can open a wormhole to another point in space within the limitations of gravity fields, dark-matter charge, etc. This Qa'Resh technology wasn't shared widely. We couldn't build another one if we wanted to. The Qa'Resh kept a close hold on this because of the very real possibility that a malfunctioning device could open up the same quantum tear that destroyed the Xaros' home galaxy—the same reason you don't let toddlers play with nuclear warheads. So once we secure the Key Hole, we will send a hacked jump engine to the Apex and destroy it."

"And why won't this bomb blast come through our galaxy?" Garret asked. "Like what happened to the Xaros' home worlds?"

"Because the Apex surrounds a captive star, there's a concentration of dark energy for the tear to feed on," Stacey said. "The dark energy fades to nothing in the intergalactic void, which is why the annihilation wave that destroyed the Xaros won't erase the entire universe. The bomb's effects won't reach our galaxy. Almost certainly it won't. We are very sure it won't."

Stacey heard officers shifting in their seats and she wished that the probe masquerading as her grandfather had briefed this part as well.

"The thing is," Stacey continued as she wiped a hand across her brow, "to keep this from becoming a suicide mission, we need *two* jump engines. Thankfully, there's another one here in system. Septon Jarilla?"

The Ruhaald stood up. He held his tentacle hands in front of his chest and formed them into a steeple as he bowed slightly at the waist.

"I render appropriate greetings," Jarilla said. His words came from a voice box on his shoulder as bubbles rose from his feeder tentacles. "My queen

113

will give you the jump engine within the *Forever Tide* as a gesture of our goodwill and to atone for our actions. We were misinformed as to Earth's intentions, which led to our poor choice in allies. Your fight against the Xaros is our fight."

The Ibarra hologram appeared next to Stacey.

"Also," the probe said through Marc Ibarra's form, "controlling the Key Hole will require a significant source of computing power. A Qa'Resh probe should be able to gain control and send the bomb to the Apex."

"But if you send the probe in our Crucible, the Xaros will swarm the Earth in an instant," Valdar said. "Will the Qa'Resh on Jupiter make a new one?"

"The probes are some of the most intricate and sublime devices in all of recorded history," the hologram snapped. "They cannot be mass-produced on a whim."

"Stacey, tell Jimmy he's bombing. I'm an asshole, not a prissy little blowhard," Ibarra said through her earpiece.

Stacey pointed at Ibarra and shushed him.

"There is another probe," Jarilla said, "on Ruhaald Prime."

"Which you'll hand over to us as well?" Valdar asked.

Jarilla's two enormous squid eyes flicked from side to side, independent of each other. "I am sorry, but that is not my queen's to give. That will be a decision for the high synod."

Stacey touched her control screen. The holos disappeared and the lights rose slightly.

"Which brings us to the next phase," Stacey said. "The Ruhaald fleet will leave Earth space and return to their home world...along with a diplomatic mission consisting of myself and the *Breitenfeld* to secure the second probe."

CHAPTER 8

Stacey walked along a thorn the width of a football field. The slight thump of her footsteps against the basalt-like material echoed through her helmet as the Crucible shifted around her. The thorns had to keep moving to keep the quantum field through the solar system out of balance, preventing the Xaros from making a sudden advance toward the Earth. The probe assured her pathway would remain steady and pose no risk.

Still...the thought of being crushed beneath the massive thorns like a bug against a rolling pin unsettled her.

"Would that even kill me? I got stabbed on Bastion—didn't bother me a bit. Course being flattened out into a Stacey-tortilla isn't within the design…why am I talking to myself?" She quickened her stride, mag-locking the soles of her suit against the thorn with each step.

The vac suit was an affectation; she understood that. She'd been through hard vacuum, exposed to the insane winds and radiation of Jupiter with no ill effects. A nigh-immortal body was no match for her spacer instincts, which demanded the same precautions as her old, fragile body.

Stacey touched her chest, feeling a phantom pain from the bullets that led to her unnatural state.

"Won't hurt to ask…"

The end of the thorn unraveled into loose honeycomb stalactites. Glowing omnium cubes floated in a net attached to the unfinished edge where Torni—in her drone form—worked feverishly with her many stalks to convert omnium into the remainder of the piece of the Crucible.

"Not so different, she and I…" Stacey's eyes traced the long arch of the Crucible, trying to remember just where she and Torni had landed all those years ago when Earth's last surviving fleet

117

attacked the Crucible.

A vibration travelled up Stacey's legs. She took a half step back, hands raised to fight as Malal floated up from the construction effort and stopped level with her. The ancient entity's face was blank, gentle fractal patters rolled across his surface.

+Your soul is cold.+

Stacey felt Malal's words as a tiny thrum against her body. She matched it to send, +Will she hear us?+

+No. You've chosen to ascend from your primitive form. Curious.+

+This wasn't a choice, Malal, and the more I think about it, the more I wish…you don't even care. That's not why I'm here. The Qa'Resh have run tests on your codex, the data we recovered from your vault. There's an issue.+

Malal bobbed ever so slightly.

+We can use it to access the gateways,+ Stacey said, +but not the drones. If we destroy the Apex, it won't amount to much if all the drones across the galaxy keep to their base programming. The drones will broadcast any and all evidence of intelligent life to each other and attack until xenocide is complete. They self-replicate faster than damn rabbits too.+

Malal didn't respond.

+The Qa'Resh would appreciate your input,+ Stacey said. She peered over the edge to Torni.

+That one is broken,+ Malal said. +The kill function she carried is gone. You would still sacrifice her if you could, wouldn't you? My...those of your kind carrying the name 'Ibarra' will grow to rule much, if you survive at all.+

+Being aware of a course of action is not the same as taking it,+ Stacey snapped. +The Qa'Resh think you might have a solution.+

Malal turned and floated away.

+Your bargain was to help us defeat the Xaros, Malal!+ Stacey's words were enough to stop Malal in his tracks. +If we go extinct in the next year, or the next thousand years, it doesn't matter. The Qa'Resh won't keep their end of the deal.+

Malal's body twisted inside out, his blank face swarming with fractal patterns as he came straight for Stacey.

+You think yours is the first to try to hold leverage over me? You think the Xaros are the only empire I've had to wait out? The Fa'lun Hegemony crumbled to dust as I watched. I sat back as a memetic virus corrupted the hive minds of the Obernalli androids and drove all nine quadrillion of them into insanity. The Xaros will come and the Xaros will go. Don't think that you are my last chance at revenge.+

+But you've never been so close to that revenge, have you?+ Stacey asked. +We have your door, your last step to ascension. But if you want it, you'll have to help us destroy the drones and the Apex.+

Malal waved his hand toward the thorn next to Stacey. Dust rose and whirled around Malal's palm. It formed into a small city of gleaming spires connected by a spider web of crystalline bridges.

+There was one...more talented than I. She led the campaign to have me exiled after I laid the groundwork for our immortality. She was the only one that ever beat me,+ Malal said.

+We really don't have time for another snipe

hunt, Malal. The Xaros will be here in months and—
+

+Your very narrow path to survival leads
here. Bring me to this city and I will have the tools I
need to end your fear of the drones. You will take me
to the door before I hand over that power.+

+What are you talking about? The Qa'Resh
said they will—+

+I will go to the Sletari with you. I will obtain
what you desire. Then you will take me to my reward
without delay. Then our bargain will be complete.+
Malal reached toward her and his fingers passed
through her visor and caressed her cheek. +Earth will
know what you did. They will know your crimes, all
of your sins.+

Malal withdrew and sank back toward Torni.

****

Captain Valdar leaned back from the holo
tank on his bridge and crossed his arms over his
chest. The Ruhaald ships moved one by one through
a cordon of human warships to the center of the

Crucible. The alien vessels took void anchor only a few tens of yards from each other.

"Rail batteries one and two locked on," Utrecht said from the gunner's station. "They step out of line and they're fish in a barrel. Macro cannons on Luna's Grimaldi crater have their finger on the trigger as well."

"They're getting off easy," said Ericson, the ship's executive officer. "Show up, destroy our ships, threaten our cities and our families. Then we practically give them a pat on the back on the way out."

"Politics makes for strange bedfellows," Valdar said. "War, stranger still. The three Chinese pilots we picked up after that skirmish worked out well enough."

"At least the Chinese are people. What're the Ruhaald? Shrimp or something?" Ericson asked.

"More like squid...but with arms and legs," Valdar said. "Amphibian squids that can walk around and—sometimes I miss fighting the Chinese. I admit it."

A hologram of Marc Ibarra popped up in the

holo tank.

"Wormhole gate to Ruhaald Prime will form in twenty minutes. Please take your assigned position within the iris," Ibarra said and vanished.

"Not much for banter," Valdar said. "Conn!"

"Aye aye, sir!" Ensign Geller said.

Valdar felt a rumble as the *Breitenfeld*'s engines came to life.

"XO, set the ship to battle stations once we're in position," Valdar said. "We'll maintain that until we're sure the Ruhaald welcome is as pleasant as promised. I'm a little short on trust these days."

The main door to the bridge opened and Hale, clad in his battle armor, entered, followed by Stacey and an armed Ranger with his visor down.

"Stacey, always a pleasure to have you aboard," Valdar said with a tight jaw. A chill went through his body as she neared. Valdar looked closely at her face, his brows furrowed in confusion at her appearance.

"Yes," Stacey said, "I'm a little different than normal. This," she said, tapping a fingertip against the side of her head with a slight clink, "is how diplomacy happened on Bastion. An elegant solution to many different problems." She gave Hale a quick glance. "I'll be back to normal once this is all over."

"And how exactly will this diplomatic mission play out?" Valdar asked. "Different from sneaking around Nibiru to assassinate an alien leader, one hopes."

"The Ruhaald aren't a mono-culture like humanity became after the Xaros invasion," she said. "There are many different factions on the planet that work together only for issues of common defense. The Ruhaald ambassador on Bastion and I had a good working relationship until—"

"Soldier, get your finger off that trigger," Hale said to the Ranger.

The Ranger glanced down at his gauss rifle where he did indeed have his finger on the trigger. Hale knew that proper trigger discipline was ingrained into every soldier, sailor and Marine before they ever touched a weapon. *How is an elite soldier like the Ranger making this mistake?*

"Your weapon is off safe as well," Hale growled and reached for the Ranger. He clamped down on the soldier's wrist then pulled his hand back with a yelp. Hale shook his hand quickly and hissed through his teeth.

"He's cold," Hale said.

The bridge crew had their eyes on the altercation; more than one had hands on their side arms.

"Perhaps your ready room?" Stacey asked.

"Follow me," Valdar said as he backed toward the small door at the rear of the bridge. He walked quickly into his office and stood behind his chair, drawing his pistol and keeping it hidden from Stacey and the Ranger as they entered.

The Ranger held his rifle out to Hale, who snatched it away, removed the magazine and tossed it onto a slim bed against a far wall.

"I told you this getup was a mistake," the Ranger said to Stacey. He removed his helmet with a quick twist, revealing a middle-aged looking Marc Ibarra within.

"Ibarra," Valdar said.

"In the flesh. Such as it is."

Valdar snapped the pistol over the chair and

aimed it at Ibarra's forehead.

"Now, now, don't be hasty," Ibarra said. His eyes darted to the side and saw Hale's pistol also aimed at his head. "Your bullets won't accomplish much other than go bouncing willy-nilly, and that will be bad only for the two of you."

"Captain," Stacey said as she held her hands up to try to calm the two men, "this isn't going to help our mission."

"Son of a bitch, you've got some nerve stepping foot on my ship after what you've put us all through," Valdar said. "How long have you been walking around? Got tired of hiding on the Crucible where no one could get to you?"

"Times change. Things don't work out as you like," Ibarra shrugged. "Neither Stacey nor I want this setup, but here we are. This wasn't by choice— believe me. If I go walking around Phoenix like this, half the people will react just like you did."

"My wife," Valdar said, tapping the side of his thumb against his pistol to set it to HIGH power, "my children. They're dead because you left them behind on Earth for the Xaros."

126

"I had the chance to save the human race at great cost," Ibarra said. "I was on Earth when it ended. I heard the screams. Saw the Xaros burn through every last city but Phoenix. My wife and children died and then I…passed on. I'll get what I deserve one way or another. For the sake of our mission, let's not forget that the Xaros are coming again and our best hope for survival means going to the Ruhaald and playing nice. Put that gun away."

"Why are you on my ship?" Valdar asked, keeping his pistol leveled at Ibarra.

"I've been stuck inside that probe for thirty fucking years." Ibarra pointed at a wall. "Now here's my chance to go see something other than the inside of the Crucible and I think I've earned a hall pass."

"And all the doughboys on the Crucible would try to rip him apart at first glance," Stacey said. "Our appearance is so off that it triggers their aggression response."

Valdar lowered his pistol. Hale followed suit.

"This is my ship," Valdar said. "You will follow my orders. Now get to your assigned quarters and don't come out unless I say otherwise."

"But when we—"

"My ship!" Valdar slammed a palm against his desk. "You comply or I'll have you thrown out of an airlock with a propellant gun and you can float back to your hole on the Crucible."

"Fine." Ibarra waved a hand at the rifle Hale'd taken from him. "Give me back that gun."

"No," Hale deadpanned.

"Can we at least keep my presence here off the books?" Ibarra asked.

"Put that helmet on and keep your head down for the rest of your stay." Valdar pointed to the door.

"Captain," Geller said through an intercom, *"we're in position. Void combat conditions set in two minutes."*

"I'll be right out." Valdar jammed a finger at the door again.

Ibarra donned his helmet and gave Valdar a bent-handed—and very wrong—salute.

CHAPTER 9

Valdar squeezed his eyes shut as the blazing light of the wormhole faded away. He opened an eye as color returned to his bridge. His crew, who'd been through more than one wormhole, recovered quickly and gave updates through the bridge IR system.

"All weapons batteries fully charged and awaiting instructions."

"Flight deck reports ready condition one. Birds in the void within thirty seconds of release."

"Hull integrity normal."

"We're at high anchor over a planet." Geller looked up from a screen, a smile on his face. "It's…it looks a lot like Earth."

"Any word from the Ruhaald?" Valdar asked Ericson.

"Nothing yet, sir. Most of their ships are still coming through. No sign of the *Forever Tide*," she said.

"Stay frosty, everyone. They haven't rolled out the welcome mat for us just yet," Valdar said. A video feed opened on a screen attached to his armrest. A world of deep blue oceans and long bands of green continents appeared. A pair of hurricanes roiled near the equator. A slice of the world was at night and thick patches of city lights clung to unseen coastlines and harbors.

"Sir," Utrecht said, waving to the captain, "three cruiser analogues on an intercept course with us. Coming in fast."

"Put it in the tank." Valdar unbuckled from his captain's chair and went to the holo tank where his ship appeared as a blue triangle. Green icons of Ruhaald ships arriving from Earth popped up several hundred kilometers away. Three red arrows followed a dashed-line path toward his ship.

Stacey struggled out of a chair bolted to the wall and joined Valdar at the tank.

"This isn't right," she said. "The Ruhaald ships were supposed to come through first...and we were supposed to be a lot closer together."

"We can figure out the screwup later." Valdar zoomed the tank in on the three approaching cruisers, all studded with weapons batteries. "You're the diplomat. Get them to back off before they learn what rail cannons taste like."

Stacey swiped fingers over a forearm screen. "Septon Jarilla, this is the *Breitenfeld*. Request you tell the welcoming party we're friendly and to stand down." There was no answer. She reached into the holo tank and zoomed in on the Ruhaald ships that'd come from Earth. The *Forever Tide* was missing.

She bit her lip and double-tapped a battle cruiser, the *Endless Depths*. A working icon popped up next to it, then switched to an error.

"Why can't I open a channel to the Ruhaald ships?" Stacey called out to the bridge crew.

"All their ships are radio silent," Ericson said. "Want a wide-band transmission to the three ships on their way over here?"

"They'll enter weapons' range in five

131

minutes," Utrecht called out.

Stacey looked at Valdar and shrugged.

"Hail the cruisers," Valdar said. "Tell Gall she may have to launch into hot space. Helm, take us forward at half speed. No reason to be a sitting duck if we have the choice."

"Aye aye." The commo officer tapped out commands on her workstation.

The cruisers adjusted their intercept course immediately. Two long minutes passed as the *Breitenfeld*'s hails went unanswered.

Then, a green dot appeared next to the center cruiser. A screen popped up with a Ruhaald floating in a sapphire-blue tank of water. More of the Ruhaald aquatic caste swam in the background.

Bubbles and squeaks came through channel.

Stacey tapped the Qa'Resh translation box on her shoulder and said, "This is Stacey Ibarra, chief diplomat of the Atlantic Union delegation. From Earth. There seems to be some technical difficulty. Our mission is peaceful. Please adjust your course."

The Ruhaald leaned toward the camera.

"You speak Daeadalla. I do not care for their

words. I am Scion Ciuul of the Berilla. You must be the first of the slaves. Power down your weapons and prepare to be boarded," the alien said.

"There's been some misunderstanding," Stacey said. "The Daeadalla reached a settlement with Earth. We are not slaves. Septon Jarilla will explain that to you," she said as she looked at the fleet of ships that had come through the now-shrinking wormhole, "once he arrives. Which will be any moment now."

Ciuul pulled back from camera. Limbs tipped with flippers swung between its body.

"The Daeadalla promised slaves. Your ship holds a jump engine. I claim it for the Berilla. You will stand by to be boarded. Resistance will be punished." The channel cut out.

"No, no, no," Stacey repeated the word and tapped her forearm screen rapidly, trying to reopen the connection.

"I knew this was a mistake." Valdar shook his head. "Engine room, prep an immediate jump back to Earth."

"Love to, Captain, but there's a fluctuation in the

quantum field that's driving the engines batty," Lieutenant Commander Levin said through the IR. *"Get us a couple hundred thousand miles from the planet and we'll be good to go."*

"Helm, turn us about. Engines at best speed." Valdar pointed a finger at Stacey. "You tell those other squids that they have exactly thirty seconds to break off before I start shooting."

"I would if I could, sir, but they're actively jamming every frequency I try using."

"Gall, this is Valdar. I want your fighters to run interdiction until we—"

A pair of jagged bolts of red energy snapped past the bridge.

"Guns!" Valdar slapped a red button on the holo tank and his command chair turned around and slid forward on rails. "Target the engines on the center ship and fire when ready."

Bursts of light splashed across the *Breitenfeld*'s hull, as if a thunderstorm raged high above.

Two of the threatening icons in the holo tank blinked. A red X appeared over them both as the two destroyed ships veered off course.

"Guns, belay that order," Valdar said.

A massive Ruhaald ship sped past the *Breitenfeld*'s prow, disgorging arrowhead-shaped fighters by the dozen from hangars spread across its centerline.

"Captain Valdar," Septon Jarilla said as he appeared in the holo tank, "there is a blood feud between the Berilla and my people, one that's gone on for many centuries. Your arrival and mission are not going to plan."

"You don't say." Valdar's pounding heart and adrenaline-tense muscles didn't relax as more Daeadalla ships from the septon's fleet formed a protective cordon around the *Breitenfeld*.

"My queen is in contact with the synod now," Jarilla said. "The negotiations for your presence on the surface shouldn't take much time." The alien's image vanished.

"We have to negotiate to negotiate," Stacey said. "Wonderful."

"Why is this a surprise to you? Also, why didn't you mention all these blood feuds before we arrived? If there's something affecting the safety of

135

my crew and my ship, I expect to know about it long before the shooting starts," Valdar said.

"I know the basics about the Ruhaald through their ambassador on Bastion. The probe back on Earth didn't carry any information on them—a security precaution in case the probe was ever compromised. Can't hack data that's not in a system. But Darcy—"

"Darcy?"

"Their ambassador. I can't pronounce her name without gills so I called her something else. Don't judge me. Darcy mentioned the political situation on her home world was complicated, but we never got into specifics. We spent most of our time trying to figure out the Xaros problem. None of the ambassadors talked about home that much. Kind of a faux pas."

"How are you going to negotiate if you don't know anything about the Ruhaald?"

"We know enough. They're terrified. Terrified of the Xaros drone maniple heading straight for them that's less than a decade away. That's why they sided with the Vishrakath plot to extort the proccie tech from us even though I told Darcy we'd fight beside them once their fleets helped defend Earth." Stacey tugged at her bottom lip. "Of course, we also know they can't be trusted."

Valdar grunted. "I'm glad you and Ibarra are here. If this blows up in our faces, you'll be sure to see it."

"Captain?" The communications officer waved a hand in the air. "Incoming transmission from the planet."

"In the tank."

"It's for Ms. Ibarra, sir."

"Tank, please." Stacey rubbed her gloved hands together. "Progress!"

The grainy image of a Ruhaald with overly long feeder tentacles and a light-pink sheen to its skin formed in the tank.

"I render appropriate greetings, Stacey Ibarra," the alien said.

"Are you... *Thrakkorzog?* No, *Lakkidivog.* Wait—"

"Darcy. I am glad you escaped Bastion. The implications of your arrival are already spreading

137

across the planet. The peace I brokered between the queens to face the Xaros is falling apart. There will be a full-scale war between most of the factions by nightfall," she said.

"Just because we showed up?" Stacey asked, her face falling into a despondent frown.

"Why is *Forever Tide*'s jump engine missing? That was our only hope of escape from the Xaros. The other queens will be furious when they learn of this," Darcy said.

"Back up—how can we stop the war? We didn't come here to pick sides or shoot anyone."

"I can use what little influence I have left to call a synod. I will send you the coordinates. You may bring a single shuttle. Come unarmed." Darcy's transmission cut out.

"Progress," she said to Valdar with a quick nod.

"I can't risk this ship for you," the captain said. "The jump engine is vital to the attack on the Apex. If things go south down there or the Ruhaald make another play for the *Breitenfeld*, we are leaving. With or without you."

"I understand, and I don't blame you," she said. "I might have a few hours to discuss things with Jarilla before—" A pulsating beacon appeared on a coastline adjacent to a narrow sea, along with a timer promising only a few hours until zero. "Or I can run down to a Mule and leave right now. I'm not going to catch a break today, am I?"

CHAPTER 10

The Mule's ramp lowered onto a beach of pale yellow sand. Hale held a hand over his visor to block the powerful rays coming off the twin suns low in the sky. Thunderstorms raged in the distance, the roof of the storm clouds stretched into anvil-shapes by high altitude winds. An ATMO beacon blinked against his faceplate.

The ramp bit into the sand and Standish ran past Hale. In full combat armor, the Marine's boots stomped against the ramp with a *clang* then thumped into the loose ground. He kicked up a spray of tiny crystalline granules.

"Woo! Private First Class Standish is the first human to step foot on Planet Squid." He banged a

140

fist against his chest. "Let's see them edit *that* out of the history books. First man to greet the Karigole. First man on Anthalas. Now Squid Town."

"Should we leave him behind?" Cortaro asked Hale.

"Tempting..." Hale went down the ramp and grabbed Standish by the back of the neck. The young Marine stopped celebrating instantly.

Stacey and Cortaro joined them on the beach. Sapphire-blue waves crashed against the surf for miles up and down the coastline. Mountains rose behind them. A meandering road cut a line across the range, the glint of sunlight off scattered dome-shaped structures offered another sign of civilization.

Hale glanced at a map on his forearm screen.

"This is the place," he said. "Made it with a couple minutes to spare."

"Doesn't really look like a place to have a nice sit-down discussion, does it?" Stacey asked. She wore a light, skintight vac suit instead of combat armor like her Marines escort. She didn't want to look threatening to the Ruhaald but the rest of the shore party needed to convey the threat of violence if pressed, even if they didn't carry any weapons.

"Atmo pressure is good, same with gravity," Cortaro said as he swiped his screen. "Way too much CO2 in the air, barely any free oxygen. We can breathe this stuff, but still suffocate."

"So much for opening a resort on this place," Standish said. "Plus, I doubt the natives are friendly."

Stacey put her hands on her hips. "I'm not a Ruhaald synod but from what Torni and the Iron Hearts saw of that queen on the *Forever Tide*, I was expecting something a bit more...regal. And then...there's something in the water."

She pointed to the waves.

Hale's hands flexed, wishing for his absent rifle. He stepped in front of Stacey as a pale shape the size of a small fishing boat sped just beneath the waves toward them. A chill bit through his upper arm. He glanced back and saw Stacey cowering behind him, her hands gripping him just above the elbow. Her touch was uncomfortable even through his armor, but he didn't pull away.

A submarine with a pearl and ivory hull reared out of the water and slid onto the beach. A membrane slid open as seawater poured down the exterior. A stoop-shouldered Ruhaald with pink skin came to the opening and gestured at Stacey.

"That's Darcy." She let Hale go and removed her helmet, shaking her heavy hair out with a swish of frost.

"Whoa, wait a minute." Standish reached for her and caught the helmet when she tossed it to him.

"Hard to show sincerity behind a helmet," she said. "Plus, I don't need to breathe when I'm like this. Do you want to come, Standish?"

"No, he doesn't." Hale put a hand against Stacey's back and gave her a slight press forward. He turned to Cortaro and said, "You get the recall from Valdar, you don't wait around. Got me?"

"Sir, I don't know how we could even find you once you get in that thing. Other than that, we'll squat and hold until you two get back," Cortaro said.

Hale gave him a nod and caught up to Stacey.

"Thanks for coming, Ken," she said as they walked toward the waiting vessel. "I feel a lot better doing this with you here."

"I don't have my rifle, my sidearm or my

143

grenades. This armor can swim as well as an anchor. Not sure what good I can do for you," he said. "Least I'm not completely useless." He gave his right arm, the one with the Ka-Bar combat knife in the forearm housing, an exaggerated swing. "You should have brought armor to escort you."

"The Ruhaald specifically forbade the armor from coming along. I think they're afraid of Elias."

"You didn't see what he did to them on Earth." A shiver went through his body as the memory of crushed alien bodies and Elias' gore-covered armor came back to him. Hale had never seen armor that shied away from battle, but sometimes he feared that Elias actually enjoyed the carnage.

"Ken, just so you know," Stacey said through his IR earpiece, her lips didn't move as she spoke. *"I have an override code for the Ruhaald's probe that* might *work. If it takes, the probe will shoot straight for the* Breitenfeld. *With only one probe we can't attack the Apex without leaving the Earth vulnerable to the Xaros opening a wormhole right on top of the planet. The override code is our last resort down here. I transmit it and things will go very bad for us down here."*

144

"You might have mentioned this sooner," Hale said.

Stacey stopped a few steps away from the submarine.

"Mentioned what?" Stacey said out loud as she waved to Darcy.

Darcy's bulbous head turned from side to side, looking at her with each wide black eye.

"You are different than I remember," the Ruhaald said.

"This is my simulacrum body, from Bastion. I escaped the Xaros attack with the Qa'Resh after Wexil and his bunch of traitorous scum locked Pa'lon and I in the transfer chamber." A sneer went across Stacey's face.

A small ramp extended from the opening into the sand. Hale went up first. He got through the opening...and found himself standing on a bare deck with Darcy and nothing else. He reached out and touched an invisible wall.

"Projection screens," Darcy said. She was two feet taller than Hale and almost twice as wide. As she sidestepped away from him, Hale caught a glimpse of sucker pads beneath her feet as she moved.

Hale reached back and helped Stacey up by the hand. His bones stung with cold, like he'd forgotten to wear gloves during a winter's night.

"Well, this a neat trick," Stacey said as she looked around.

"The synod is waiting for us." Darcy went to the fore of the submarine and wiggled the tips of her long tentacles in a holo field. Deep gashes ran down her back, each filled with a ruby-red substance that looked like coral.

"You're hurt," Stacey said.

The submarine shifted forward with the barest hint of inertia and slipped beneath the waves. Light played through the wavy ceiling and glinted off a school of rainbow-colored fish the size of Hale's finger. A pack of crustaceans with pearl shells skittered across the sea floor.

"The queens are agitated," Darcy said, "some more so than others. It was not easy to get this audience."

"You owe me an explanation," Stacey said. "You promised the Ruhaald would help fight off the

Xaros, not stab us in the back the first chance you got. What happened?"

"I made that agreement in good faith with you, and the Naroosha, on Bastion. But when I came back home, the Naroosha fleet was already here. Their leader, this Ordona, promised the synod their own Crucible gate, their own procedurally generated humans who would fight without compulsion or regard for their own safety. I pleaded with the synod to refuse, to trust in your promise to fight alongside us when the time came."

"Then your synod chose humanity to be their slaves instead of their friends," Stacy said, her words tinged with hatred.

"We are not a unified race," Darcy said. "Warring against each other is essential for a queen's brood to grow stronger. The procedural humans were something they could count on. It is not in the synod's nature to trust each other. They agreed to the Naroosha's, and the Vishrakath's plan. Then our probe, my companion for so long, was compromised. I couldn't go back to warn you."

"Bastion is gone," Stacey said. The water

darkened as the sub sank deeper and deeper. "The Xaros aren't afraid to use their own wormhole technology anymore. They could be here any time they choose."

"We received a garbled warning from the Vishrakath through the probe. Our attempts to disrupt quantum space through our probe are evidently useless," Darcy said.

"So that's why our jump-in system went haywire." Hale squinted at a distant shadow moving through the darkness.

"Your people betrayed us," Stacey said. "If circumstances were different, we may have come here with a lot more ships and a lot fewer friendly words, but we need the Ruhaald to drive a stake through the Xaros' heart and win this war. I need you to help me convince the synod to help us."

"That the *Breitenfeld* accepted Jarilla's surrender and spared his queen will help convince the others that humanity can be trusted. There is an issue...you are Hale?"

The two humans exchanged a quick look.

"That's right," he said.

"You encountered one by the name of Tuk."

"We've met." Hale's hands squeezed into fists as anger boiled out of his heart.

"Tuk had the chance to kill you. His decision to let you live has proven...difficult for us."

"That bastard murdered soldiers right in front of me for some vendetta I still don't understand. What does that have to do with anything?"

"The gestalt chose Tuk as the new scion, but his metamorphosis proved incomplete. You were responsible for the death of many Ruhaald, correct?"

"It was a war. I did what I had to and only regret that I couldn't save more men and women from the Ruhaald."

"I do not blame you," Darcy said. She turned her head to the abyss surrounding the submarine. Her long feeder tentacles flicked toward a tiny point of light that emerged from the distance. "Our biology demands constant strife. The blood feud did not end on Earth as Tuk thought it would. Witnessing so many dead at your hand pushed him into a rage that has infected many of the Daeadalla. His queen can suppress it through her pheromones, but that

149

aggression has spread to other pods and other queens."

"I knew we should have brought Elias down here," Hale said.

"So what does that mean?" Stacey asked.

"I don't know yet." The Ruhaald ambassador directed the submarine toward the light. As the light grew stronger, Hale made out an elongated tear with jagged edges.

"There's your Qa'Resh probe," Stacey said.

"It is where we will find the synod," Darcy said. The submarine settled against the seabed just beneath the probe, its pale light illuminating gray mud and swathes of rocky outcrops in a circle around the submarine.

"So we just wait here for...oh my god." Stacey backed into Hale as a Ruhaald queen came out of the darkness, dwarfing the submarine. Her tentacles, thicker than a millennia-old sequoia, undulated toward them.

Stacey whimpered as the leathery tip caressed the invisible walls of the sub. Darcy pressed her hand against the wall and seawater bubbled out from her touch. A whiff of orange dust came off the queen's tentacle as it passed over Darcy's hand.

"We have no words for 'hello,'" the ambassador said. "We exchange pheromones that convey our mood, vitality and even our queen mother's breeding cycle. That is the Daeadalla matriarch…and she is afraid."

"Any particular reason?" Stacey asked. "Maybe there are giant sharks down here. There could be sharks? Right, Ken? Maybe even a kraken or—"

Hale put a hand on her shoulder to stop her nervous babbling.

"Each queen has their own fleet." Darcy took her hand from the wall and the trickle of water stopped. "Most of the fleets were spread across the system. Now that we know the Xaros could be here at the time of their choosing, all ships are returning to protect the home world. The fear…the hostility…there will be open warfare in the skies and beneath the seas."

The sound of whale song punctuated by clicks washed over the sub, sending a gentle vibration through the walls. Another queen appeared out of the darkness. Then another. And another.

Light from the probe glinted off wide eyes all around the submarine.

A Ruhaald with a powerful build and legs ending in flippers swam up to the submarine. Hale took in the alien's effortless grace as it stopped just above the submarine and held a tentacled hand up to the probe.

"That is Jarilla," Darcy said. "He will begin the synod."

Jarilla drew an obsidian knife from his belt and ran the blade along his forearm. Blood welled up from the wound and lingered in the dark water. The septon raised his flippers and wafted the blood around and toward the assembled queens.

"Do we have to do that too?" Stacey asked, giving Hale a sheepish look, "because then that's all you." She looked at her hand and wiggled her fingers. "I'm not exactly sure what's even under here."

"You bring us humans," a regal woman's voice came from the probe, fluctuating with each syllable, "but they are not what we desired."

152

"The humans defeated the Daeadalla," a second voice said. "They offered their own throat to save their queen and now they dare return. Where is our jump engine, humans? It was our only hope to survive if the Xaros take our water."

"We took the jump engine in exchange for your fleet's release," Stacey said loudly. "You destroyed our ships. Killed our sailors. Threatened our cities. The concept of blood money is something both our species can understand."

"Then our only hope is the jump engine within your ship." A queen with red speckles over her pitch-black skin floated toward them. Her forward tentacles rose, revealing a curved beak that looked like it could bite through Hale in an instant. "We can flee to another star. Stay a few years ahead of the Xaros."

"And what will you do when you run out of stars? The Xaros will swallow this entire galaxy. You might buy some time by running, but they will find out where you are and destroy you at the time of their choosing. The Xaros are already moving to Earth again. But there's another way." Stacey sidestepped and looked the queen in one of her bulbous eyes.

"One that will end the Xaros threat for good. No need for fleets—human or Ruhaald. That will only stem the tide for a time."

"You have our attention," the voice came through the probe with a clarion call.

"We can destroy the Xaros, strike them at their home, the Apex." Stacey pointed at the Ruhaald ambassador. "She helped me find it in the void beyond the galactic rim. It exists and we can reach it, but to do that we need your probe...and your fleet."

A cacophony of voices came through the probe. Its surface went wild with color as bubbles and tentacles erupted from the surrounding queens.

"I may have asked too much," Stacey said to Hale.

Darcy's eyes flit back and forth, each moving independently of the others.

"There is much fear," the ambassador said. "They believe the probe is the only thing keeping the Xaros away for now...they think the Naroosha might send ships to help, or the other races aligned with the Vishrakath."

"The Naroosha will not save you!" Stacey

shouted. The din died down as queens pressed toward the sub slowly. "The Qa'Resh gave one—and only one—jump engine to a few of races. The Naroosha ship that jumped to Bastion was destroyed. I saw it with my own eyes. The Vishrakath are hundreds of light-years from here. No one is coming to save you but *us!*"

"You cannot be trusted." A queen with yellow and black mottled skin floated near. "You, the one in the shell, you were granted a *kitithrak* to end a blood feud. You did not accept. You laid a trap that led to the death of many warriors." The queen spread her tentacles, revealing a Ruhaald warrior with limbs meant for walking on solid ground. His skin bore stretch marks, as if his broad shoulders and trunk-like legs had grown in overnight.

Tuk.

"Hale, remain calm," Darcy said.

"You think I gave a rat's ass about your ways?" Hale advanced toward Tuk, stopping at the edge of the sub's floor. "He was murdering prisoners. He led an attack that killed dozens of people *after* the cease-fire. I acted to save lives. If he didn't want to die, he should have stayed in whatever moist hole you call a home."

"Not calm, Ken." Stacey shook her head. "Not calm at all."

"Many of my brood are still buried beneath a mountain," Tuk said, stepping forward slowly through the water. "Their bodies will rot in the soil. Their flesh is lost to the brood!" Yellow flecks of dust came off Tuk's gills.

Hale snarled at the Ruhaald warrior. "A leader's pride is never worth a soldier's death. You're lucky you surrendered, or I would have come back to Earth and finished what I started when I ripped your guts out at the firebase!"

Tuk slammed a fist against the sub's wall. Hale didn't flinch.

"I saw my brother die because of you," Hale said slowly and evenly.

Tentacles surrounded Tuk and drew him away.

The many-voiced argument resumed through the probe.

"Some are for us," Darcy said, "more against.

156

Tuk released an anger pheromone that's affecting the queens."

Hale went back to Stacey and opened the IR channel to her earpiece. "Do it. Do it now. They're distracted and confused."

"What do you think they'll do to us? To your Marines on the surface?"

"If we die down here but save the Earth, it'll be worth it."

"It might not work. The probe's been hacked."

"A chance is better than none."

A pair of thumps sounded through the sub. Jarilla stood on top of the ceiling, his knife clutched in one hand.

"The Daeadalla declare this synod contaminated," Jarilla said. "My queen's spawn has polluted your spirit. She demands an end to this bickering, a return to harmony so we can address the true issue, the Xaros threat."

"Blood must follow blood," the yellow and black queen said. "End the feud. End the vendetta." The synod repeated the queen's words several times.

"Hale...what have you done?" Stacey asked.

157

Jarilla swam down next to Hale and said, "Blood must follow blood, but if you fight Tuk to the death, there will be closure...restore the queens to a peaceful state."

Stacey came to the wall.

"I think everything just got a little heated," she said. "Let's take a little break before we discuss ritual killings, OK?"

"I win and you'll cooperate with us?" Hale asked Darcy.

"The logic is there to assist you, but they are too scared and angry to act rationally," she said.

"I'll do it," Hale told Jarilla. "We have no more time to waste. Bring Tuk in here."

"Not here," Jarilla said, looking up at the surface. "There is a place for this. We will leave now."

Jarilla twisted around and thumped his fists against his chest, letting out a cry that sounded like a bull sea lion's call through the sub's walls. Then he swam off into the abyss.

"There." Hale shrugged his shoulders. "Progress."

CHAPTER 11

Hale paced back and forth across a sand bar ten yards wide and four times as long. The island sat alone, surrounded by nothing but the shimmering sea and bright bands of coral as far as his eye could see. Hale wore only a skintight body glove, his armor and pseudo-muscle layer stacked neatly next to Stacey, who kept her gaze on the horizon.

Hale tightened the respirator over his nose and mouth, then fumbled with the air line running to air tanks on his lower back.

"Damn it," Hale said as he tried to swing the loose line to a grasping hand and failed.

"Here, let me." Stacey took the air line and

pressed it against a Velcro catch on the back of Hale's shoulder.

"Open the back of my suit and stuff it in there."

"Won't that pinch the line? Thought you'd want to breathe during a fight." She yanked the suit open, brushing her fingers against Hale's bare flesh as she stuffed the line inside.

"Ah! Son of a bitch!" Hale recoiled from her touch, which had left a small patch of gray frostbite next to his spine.

"Sorry!" Stacey gingerly resealed Hale's suit.

"Right where I can't scratch it too." Hale rolled his shoulders back and forth then went back to pacing. "Why are you like...that?"

"Everyone on Bastion had a body like this. It really was the only way to have so many different species able to interact in a meaningful way. What? You don't like it?"

Hale stopped. "Through all this mess, ever since the engines went haywire before we were supposed to go to Saturn and up until now, I thought you were one of us. Just another leaf in the storm your grandfather created. Now, you're too much like Marc Ibarra."

"I'll go back if I—as soon as possible. Hey, you know that old joke about who you'd want to be trapped on a desert island with?" She spread her arms to the simple strip of sand. "Was I ever on your list?"

"Something's coming." Hale's hand went to his armor. He drew his Ka-Bar knife and flipped it into a reverse grip, the flat of the blade pressed against his forearm.

A Ruhaald walked out of the ocean. Seawater ran down his body as he held up a hand to Hale, who'd dropped into a fighting stance.

"That's Jarilla," Stacey said.

Hale relaxed, but only slightly.

Jarilla spoke, his voice a series of guttural barks until a box on his shoulder translated his words: "For the blood debt to end, there must be no outside interference. Weapons no longer than half an arm."

"What else?" Hale asked. "What if he gives up?"

Jarilla's head cocked to the side. "Blood will follow blood."

"First one to die loses. Simple enough." Hale turned back to Stacey and brought his mouth close to her ear and whispered, "If I lose, you trigger the probe. Understand?"

"I'm not worried because you're going to win. Right?"

"Really wish we'd brought Elias down here." Hale turned around and saw Tuk at the other end of the island. The Ruhaald was bare-chested, his lower body covered by thin leather leggings embroidered in a language Hale had no idea how to read. A serrated blade in Tuk's hand looked like it was made up of shark teeth melded together.

Tuk expelled a gout of water from beneath his feeder tentacles, then the warrior pointed one of his many fingers at Hale and grunted out a few words.

Jarilla backed toward Tuk's side of the island. "He said—"

"I don't care." Hale took off running.

Tuk braced, surprised at Hale's aggressive move, then charged at Hale. Tuk grunted like a bull and raised his knife high.

Hale slowed down as Tuk picked up speed.

The Marine bent down and scooped up a handful of
sand and flung it into Tuk's face as Hale sidestepped a
lunging strike. Tuk roared and slashed his blade
blindly as his other hand brushed grit away from his
mouth and eyes.

Hale swung his blade up and slashed Tuk
across the knife arm. Blood arced into the air, leaving
deep red drops across the sand. Hale lunged at Tuk's
midsection but Tuk parried aside his blade. Hale
caught a fist just below his eyes that rocked him back.

Blood trickled down from a small cut.

Hale switched his blade to a reverse grip and
circled around Tuk, who didn't seem bothered by the
bleeding gash along his arm. The Ruhaald backed up
then jabbed at Hale with his knife. Hale estimated the
blow would fall more than a foot short, but he
brought his knife hand up as a precaution. His eyes
widened in surprised as Tuk's finger-tentacles
elongated, covering the empty space in the blink of an
eye. Tuk's blade bounced off Hale's, ripping a small
tear on Hale's forearm.

The Marine ducked and rushed forward,
trying to get into the alien's guard before he could

recover from his strike. Hale's shoulder thumped into Tuk's midsection and sent him reeling backward. Hale brought his blade up and felt it bite as it passed Tuk's face. The tips of two feeder tentacles landed at Hale's feet.

Tuk's other arm swept out and landed a glancing blow against the top of Hale's head, then he caught Hale by the wrist of his knife hand and yanked Hale off-balance. Hale rolled with his newfound momentum and twisted out of Tuk's grip. A kick slammed into Hale's back and sent him sprawling into the sand.

Hale rolled to the side, missing a strike from Tuk's knife that would have pinned him to the sand, and lashed out, jamming the tip of his blade into Tuk's shoulder. The Ruhaald backhanded Hale's arm and knocked the blade loose. Hale sprang to his feet, blade leveled at the alien warrior.

Blood trickled down Tuk's face from the severed feeder tentacles. Tuk inhaled deeply and bellowed a war cry.

Hale motioned to Tuk with his free hand.

"Come on, you ugly fuck, I ain't here to play."

Tuk leapt at Hale and the Marine ducked to the side, stabbing as his opponent went past in a blur, but he hit nothing.

Tuk landed poorly, his back to Hale, and Hale charged, his knife at his hip, ready to strike. Hale bent at the waist, dodging a wild blow from Tuk, then rammed his blade into Tuk's midsection, right where a human's heart would be. Tuk let out a yelp.

The alien grabbed Hale's knife arm as Hale savagely twisted his weapon. Tuk tried to stab at Hale, but the Marine blocked the blow with his forearm and clamped down on Tuk's thin wrist.

Hale and Tuk struggled for a moment, their eyes locked in hate, then Tuk reared his head back and slammed his forehead against Hale's mouth. The blow split Hale's lips against his teeth and dislodged his respirator.

Hale ripped his blade away and backpedaled. As he fumbled with his only source of air, he saw the glint of a blade. Tuk's knife ripped across his arm and slashed deep into his chest. A muffled scream came through Hale's clenched jaw.

A kick slammed into Hale's thigh and

knocked him to a knee. Tuk's fist broke Hale's nose
with an audible snap and sent the Marine onto his
back.

Hale struggled to get a breath of useless air
through the blood pouring down his face and throat.
Tuk stepped over Hale, his serrated knife held high.
Tuk fell to his knees and pinned Hale beneath his
bulk as he plunged the blade toward Hal's chest.

Hale got an arm up to block. Tuk's blade sank
into Hale's forearm and pierced through the other
side. The tip of Tuk's blade, red with Hale's blood,
stopped just inches from Hale's face. Hale braced his
knife arm against his impaled limb to stop Tuk's
blade.

Hale's own bloody knife flashed in the
sunlight, but he couldn't strike without giving Tuk all
the chance he needed to kill Hale.

Against the roar of blood through his ears, his
lungs burning for oxygen, he heard his brother's voice
calling his name.

Hale twisted his body aside and got the elbow
of his knife hand braced against his other wrist. He
had a few precious inches to work with and ripped his

knife across Tuk's wrist. The Ka-Bar severed the Ruhaald's hand with a spurt of blood.

Tuk reeled back, clutching his bleeding wrist against his chest.

Hale got to his feet, his vision tunneling from lack of air. His left hand fell to his side, Tuk's blade still embedded in his arm. Hale brought his knife high and slammed it into the base of Tuk's neck. The alien fell back and Hale went down with him.

Hale wrenched the blade free and plunged it into Tuk's chest. He ripped it free as blood poured from the wound and slammed the weapon into Tuk's chest again. Tuk pawed at Hale's face weakly, a burbling cry in the air.

Hale drove his knife into Tuk's skull, stopping when the hilt hit bone.

Hale let his knife go and took deep gulps of air that did nothing to help. He grabbed at the back of his neck, trying to find the air line as his vision swam. He doubled over, his body no longer answering his demands.

A chill spread across his shoulders. Hale took a deep breath and the fire in his lungs subsided. He rolled onto his back and saw Stacey leaning over him, one hand holding his respirator to his nose and mouth.

"Ken? Can you hear me? Are you OK?"

Hale held up his left arm, the Ruhaald blade still in it with Tuk's twitching hand attached. He gagged on his own blood and turned his head aside to let it spill out onto the sand.

"The Mule with Yarrow's coming. Just hold on," Stacey said as she grabbed the hilt of the impaled blade.

"No!" Hale made a feeble swat at her. "Leave it. Take it out...bleeding...worse."

Hale got to his feet. Tuk lay in the sand, just next to the water, his blood seeping into the surf and forming a dark cloud in the salt water. A tentacle swept through the dead warrior's blood. The enormous head of a queen breached the gentle waves. Hale looked her in the eye then gestured at Tuk.

"Is it over?"

More queens came to the surface around the island.

"It is," Jarilla said as he knelt next to the dead

Ruhaald. "I feel it in the air. The conflict between them is fading away."

"The probe..." Hale's face contorted with pain as his adrenaline faded away and every last cut and bruise made itself known to him.

"If we do this," Jarilla said, "you will not leave us helpless before the Xaros?"

"The sooner you bring us the probe and lend us your fleets, the sooner this war will end," Stacey said.

"And what then? What of our worlds?" Jarilla asked.

"Let me tell you something," Hale said. "Humans. Marines. In us, you will find no better friend and no worse enemy. This is...ugh..." Hale went to a knee.

"This is your last chance to make that choice," Stacey said. She tried to keep Hale upright but he shrugged off her touch.

The whine of engines filled the air as a Mule descended to the far side of the island, sand whipping into the air as it set down. Three Marines jumped out of the cargo bay before the ramp finished descending and ran to Hale, who rolled onto his back again with a groan. The sandstorm abated as the Mule's engines went to idle.

Yarrow slid to a stop next to his captain. He pressed a canister against the cut on Hale's chest and sprayed foam into the wound. Standish grabbed Hale's impaled arm and raised it up to slow the bleeding.

Orozco braced Hale's head between his meaty forearms.

"Damn, sir," Standish said, "I'd ask what the other guy looks like but I can see for myself."

"Knife missed the ulnar artery," Yarrow said as he snapped a tourniquet strap just below Hale's elbow, "but the basilic vein wasn't so lucky. Oro, Standish, pin him down." Yarrow moved aside and braced Hale's arm against his body. "You know, sir, if you ever set foot on a planet and manage *not* to bleed all over it, that would be fine by me. On three."

Yarrow got a firm grip on the hilt of the Ruhaald blade and said, "One…"

The corpsman slid the blade out and Hale mumbled angrily.

170

"That should have hurt less." Yarrow sprayed foam into the wound then wrapped a bandage over the wound that tightened on its own. He looked up at Stacey.

"Ma'am, I need to get him back to the ship sooner than later."

"Load him up. I'll be right there." Stacey squared off against Jarilla as the Marines carried Hale away. "The probe. Now. We need your ships for the attack on Sletari."

"You would leave us defenseless?"

"The *Breitenfeld*'s jump engines can form a gate large enough for a fleet twice the size of what you brought to Earth. We'll take all we can carry and send them back here once the Apex is destroyed."

"The Daeadalla will join you. The Fashalkan as well." Jarilla picked up Tuk's knife from the sand and pressed the hilt into the dead warrior's remaining hand.

"I'm sorry it came to this," Stacey said.

"This is what we are. This is what we do. No apologies needed or accepted. I hope this is the last time our people shed each other's blood."

A sliver dash of light rose from the water and zipped to the island. Stacey looked over the probe, her eyes examining the imperfections of the probe's form.

"It's OK. I know just the people who can fix you. Let's call you...Ben." She held a palm out to the probe. It shrank and pressed itself into her hand. She closed her fist and the probe's light faded away.

"Time to go, Jarilla. The longer we delay, the harder this will get." She hurried over to the waiting Mule.

****

Hale opened his eyes and saw a bland-colored ceiling and a curtain wall. He tried to sit up, but a dull pain in his chest and arm threatened to grow intensely more uncomfortable if he kept trying. He settled back into his hospital bed and looked at the pale pink scar on either side of his forearm.

"About time," came from his right.

A man with white hair and a closely shaved

beard sat in a chair next to him. The man set aside a paperback book next to a metal cane with Chinese characters running up and down its length. He wore a gunmetal gray jumpsuit with a black Templar's cross embroidered on both shoulders.

"I'm surprised they let you sleep for so long. If it was anyone else, I suspect they'd want you out of the way so stuff could actually get done. Given your wounds, I wager they wanted to give you a little break," he said.

Tapping his chest where Tuk's blade had cut, Hale winced. He looked at his visitor, blinked hard and said, "Colonel...Carius?"

"The Iron Hearts asked me to come check on you. Elias would have come himself, but..." Carius shrugged.

"I'm still on the *Breitenfeld*. What're you doing here?"

"I remember you from armor selection. I'm surprised you don't remember my speech from day one," Carius said.

"The cadre smoked us for ten hours straight before you showed up...you spoke about leadership, having the will to win. Sorry if the specifics escape me, sir."

"Leaders lead, son. This ship is Saint Michael's spear and I will not send others to fight the dragon. Armor is the only thing that has ever killed a Xaros master. You think the Corps doesn't have a piece of the fight? The armory inside Mount Olympus can handle things while I'm gone…and I'm worried for Elias."

"He's been better. From what I've noticed."

"I remember the two of you. I had you as roommates. I hoped a bit of Elias might help get you through selection, but I didn't think you'd make it through."

"Wait, what? Elias showed up to selection little more than skin and bones. He needed three different waivers just to get into basic training. He was supposed to help me?"

"And you came to Ft. Knox fresh out of Quantico at the top of your class. You had the makings of a fine officer, but I could tell you were missing something to become armor." Carius touched his chest twice.

"But you saw it in Elias?"

"Not at first. I stuck my head into the combatives trials that first week and saw the two of you on the mat. You beat the hell out of him...but what happened next?"

"I told him to stay down." Hale looked at the backs of his hands, remembering the feel of Elias's blood on his knuckles. "I told him he was beaten and then that bastard punched me in the crotch. Cadre had to pull him off."

"I saw armor in Elias that day. I didn't see it in you. Nothing to be ashamed of. Not everyone is meant for the plugs."

"You told me as much when I was waiting for the shuttle back to Quantico. You did say you still saw great things in my future. Somehow I don't think it was this," Hale said, gesturing at the sick bay.

Carius used his cane to help him to his feet. The colonel placed his hand against the top of Hale's head.

"Now...now there is armor in you. I hope we meet on the high ground." Carius rapped his cane against the side of Hale's bed twice and left.

CHAPTER 12

First Sergeant Cortaro touched his fingertips into a small cistern of holy water and crossed himself. He took his normal seat amongst the pews of the *Breitenfeld*'s cramped chapel and bent his head in prayer.

The sound of heavy footsteps against the deck plating broke his concentration. It sounded like someone in full armor was coming toward him. He mumbled an "amen" and looked up to see Torni standing at the end of the pew. Light reflected off her shell like she was enclosed in a thin case of glass. Cracks ran along her body, but her face was almost pristine.

"Hello, Gunney—I mean First Sergeant,

sorry," she said.

"Torni, what're you doing aboard?"

"May I?" She looked at an empty space beside Cortaro.

"Please."

She sat down, the wooden bench groaning beneath her weight.

"I came aboard with the bomb that might win us the war. Malal and I built it. Quantum physics was never my strength, nor multidimensional math, but I can follow instructions well enough. Give me another jump engine and I can destroy the galaxy. Also brought the armor some specialist equipment. You know...the usual."

"Nothing you mentioned involves the chapel."

"I spent a lot of time here when the ship was stuck in deep space. Everyone but Malal was frozen in time, and Malal isn't real friendly, in case you haven't noticed. So I'd come here, asking what I was, what I should be doing."

"Did you get an answer?"

"Not really. I can't say I'm part of the church

anymore. I don't eat or drink so no communion. There are no religious authorities, no bishops, cardinals, popes or anything to make any kind of expert ruling on..." she tapped her knuckles against her metal thigh with a ring, "this."

"I used to take the church for granted. It was always there, a structure for life and spirit. Now I can't even find a *vela* with *la virgin de Guadalupe*. Guess we have to figure things out on our own for a little while."

"Torni," she said, "the flesh-and-blood Torni you knew, died on Takeni. A Xaros master made a copy of her psyche, perfect down to the last neuron, before she died. One copy got shoved into a drone and dumped through a wormhole...that's me. I really don't know if I'm Torni, if I'm her soul, maybe just some computer program that can get altered at someone's whim. I had a real connection to the Xaros, but that's broken."

"Sounds like you're waiting for someone to tell you who you are. Programs don't make decisions. People decide."

Torni looked down at her hands. "I didn't

think this would ever happen to me. Growing old and going to God was the plan, unless I died in action…which did happen. I'm just lost."

"You remember when the Chinese had us pinned down in that concrete shithole outside East Timor? We had to hold out until morning before the armor or air support could get to us. You were worried about a typhoon that was going to roll in two days later. Remember?"

"You told me to focus on the fight we're in because if we don't win, the rest doesn't matter."

"And then our chopper crashed near Darwin and we had to dodge Chinese patrols in the middle of that typhoon, and you were worried that we'd miss the submarine the Australians were sending to get us and I told you—"

"I get it, I get it. We're about to launch an offensive against the Apex. Why am I bothering with existential naval-gazing?"

"Torni, you've got a situation I don't know how to help or solve. But if we don't get through this fight with the Xaros, nothing else will matter. It's blunt, but I'm a Strike Marine First Sergeant. I don't finesse anything."

"You're right. I appreciate it. When this is all over there will be plenty of time to figure me out."

Cortaro ran his hand over his forearm screen and frowned.

"Why is Standish in the arms room this early? And why is Orozco in the wrong berthing area? You think things would get easier when you're a First Sergeant. No, you get three times as many problems. Three times the asses that need my boot and I've only got the same two feet."

"I have some more work to do on the Crucible, but I'll see you on the flight deck," Torni said.

Cortaro gave her shoulder a squeeze and left the chapel. Torni stayed in the pew, her head down.

****

Steuben walked across the *Breitenfeld*'s flight deck, each footfall of his armored boots hitting with a ring. He stopped at the open bay doors and felt a hum through his armor from the force field

180

separating the pressurized deck from the void beyond.

Captain Hale had his helmet tucked beneath an arm. He gazed out at the armada of Ruhaald and human ships, as well as the Dotok *Vorpral,* massing within the Crucible.

"First Sergeant Cortaro will complete his inspection soon," Steuben said. "Your Marines are ready for you."

Hale cocked his ear up and heard Cortaro ripping into someone.

"Give him a little longer." Hale looked over Ceres to Earth. "Are there any Karigole sayings about final battles?"

"War never ends," Steuben said. "It will wax and wane of its own cycle, but it will never leave us."

"I'm starting to realize that you all aren't real big on motivational speeches."

"You are just now accepting this?"

"Say we do beat the Xaros. What'll happen to you and your village?"

Steuben scratched a clawed fingertip over his scaly chin.

"We cannot return home. What the Toth did to my people stained the world's spirit. The gethaars would never carry another child if we went back there. Africa is a bit tame for our needs but the village thrives. There is a school. We make our own weapons. Hunt and grow our own food. It will take…a long time to return to our old strength. A very long time. Will Earth let us stay?"

"If it were up to me, I'd let you all stay as long as you needed or wanted. Once the war ends, people will want to move out of the mountain cities. We all remember homes in America, Europe, a few other places. All the culture we had through the rest of the world is essentially gone. There's room for the Karigole."

"There was an orchard near my clan's home," Steuben said, looking to his cupped hand, "*thashatok* fruit trees. Spiked rinds, deep purple flesh that tasted just like your marshmallows if picked just after sunset. My father taught me that. I would like to go home, take cuttings and see if they will grow in your soil."

"Can I go with you?"

"I would like that. Cortaro has stopped

berating Bailey for masticating gum. Shall we inspect your Marines?"

"*Our* Marines, XO." Hale snapped his helmet to his thigh and walked to the three ranks of power-armor-clad men and women waiting near a dozen drop pods. Hale returned Cortaro's salute and went to Egan in the front rank.

Egan snapped to attention and presented his weapon to Hale. Hale took it, checked the charge, ran his fingers through the magazine well, and ran an IR diagnostic on the pilot and communications specialist's suit. A double beep in Hale's earpiece told him Egan's suit was fully functional.

Hale glanced at the uplink kit strapped to Egan's side.

"Tip-top and ready to rock, sir," Egan said.

Hale handed the gauss weapon back and sidestepped to Standish. Hale found Standish's weapon impeccably clean, the grenades for his rifle's underslung launcher factory-fresh, and his three Excalibur rounds fastened to his chest harness with an extra set of ties. Hale checked the Marine's armor-to-pseudo-muscle connections and found no fault.

Standish's armor even had an almost pleasant scent to it.

A wry smile crossed Standish's lips and he wiggled his eyebrows at Hale.

"Behave yourself for the next two weeks and you might get your corporal stripes," Hale said.

"Is that a threat or a promise, sir?"

"Three weeks." Hale stepped over to Orozco.

"Staff Sergeant Orozco had two pairs of...female undergarments fastened to his weapon," Cortaro said. "They were removed. Flame hazard."

"Not mine, sir," Orozco said. "They're gifts. For luck."

"Are there more?" Hale asked.

"In my sea bag, wall locker...foot locker and I think—"

"Any more on your person?"

"No, sir!" Orozco's eyes shifted from side to side. "No."

Hale heard the double beep in his ear. He slapped Orozco on the shoulder and stepped over to Yarrow.

"I endorsed your power of attorney signing

184

over your benefits to your daughter and Lilith," he said to the corpsman has he inspected Yarrow's rifle. "I don't know why the Corps wanted me to sign a waiver allowing a Marine in a combat theater to get married, but I signed that too. Bureaucracy managed to survive the end of the world."

"Thank you, sir. Means a lot to me."

"If you're as good a husband and father as you are a corpsman, you'll do just fine."

"I wouldn't mind a little less practice. If you don't mind, sir."

"I promise nothing."

Hale handed the rifle back and went to Bailey. She wore a felt slouch hat with the left side pinned up by the Strike Marine emblem. Australia had made a number of demands before its military was integrated into the Atlantic Union; preserving their traditional headgear had been a demand, not a request. Hale wasn't positive the bush knife against her thigh was within regs, and he really didn't want to find out otherwise.

Three Excalibur rounds glowed slightly through pouches on her belt.

"You get enough range time with those?" Hale asked.

"They're a pain in the arse to fire. Too light, like I'm shooting a damn spitball. Torni says they'll rip the shit out of those big nasties. That's all I need." She smacked her gum. Her eyes went wide with shock and her head snapped to Cortaro.

The first sergeant's face went red.

Hale cleared his throat and Bailey swallowed hard.

"We are not done," Cortaro said, jabbing a knife hand toward the sniper.

Hale stepped around Bailey and went down the line to Lieutenant Jacobs.

****

Elias gripped his Excalibur blade and slashed the air at chest height. Torni had adjusted the balance point to three inches forward of the guard, just as he'd asked. He looked down the length of the crystal-clear weapon, admiring the filigree wire lattice within. The weapons were specifically designed to disrupt the

186

photonic bodies of the Xaros masters. He'd used an Excalibur to kill the General on Earth; he hoped for a similar opportunity on the Apex.

The clash of metal on metal rang across the flight deck. Suited Ar'ri, holding a mock-up of the Excalibur, sparred with Adamczyk wielding a *kopia* spear. Vladislav and Ferenz practiced thrusts with Xaros-killing versions of the Hussars' traditional weapon. The Hussars had refused to go to battle with something so mundane as a sword and insisted Torni make them proper weapons. That Torni had taken the time to accommodate the Polish armor almost made up for the time she saved Malal from Elias' grasp.

Almost.

"Sir, what're they doing?" Caas motioned to where Carius and his two Templar companions were each on one knee, facing into a circle. They held their Excalibur blades point-down on the deck, the guard pressed against their helms. The sounds of Latin spoken in unison came from the Templars.

"Tradition. They recite the Psalm before battle, then receive the chaplain's blessing."

"We don't...do that?" she asked.

"Every team is different. They do what they desire. No business of mine or ours. *Gott Mit Uns* is enough."

"You have so many ways of worship on this ship. I'm surprised everyone can get along so well. The Dotok were like that, but differing theologies led to...issues on the generation ships. The high listers discouraged religion to keep the peace. I wonder if we lost too much for the sake of harmony. My family held to the tradition of the one creator. Maybe that's why we were so low list. The creator would give out blessings to those that asked...but I've forgotten the words."

Chaplain Krohe walked onto the deck in his full vestments, carrying a small bronze cup.

"Do you think Krohe would bless my weapon?" she asked. "I don't think the creator would be too upset if I go through a human ritual. In Dotok religion, it's the thought that counts."

"He might not, but he doesn't know who's inside this armor, does he?" Elias hit his fist against his chest twice, summoning Ar'ri.

The Templars broke out of their circle and knelt in a line facing the chaplain. The Hussars fell in beside them. Elias and the Iron Hearts finished the line. The ten armor soldiers knelt to one knee, blades and spear tips down, weapons pressed to their helms.

Chaplain Krohe said a prayer then made the sign of the cross. He dipped his fingertips in holy water and flicked drops onto Carius' weapon.

Carius put both hands on the hilt.

"Non nobis, Domine, non nobis sed monini Tuo da gloriam," the colonel said.

"Elias...do I have to say that?" Ar'ri asked through a private IR channel.

"Just stay quiet," Elias said.

The chaplain moved down the line, repeating the blessing until he got to Elias.

"I haven't seen you in a while," Krohe said. "We've missed you."

Elias touched a palm against his breastplate. "No one has seen me for a long time. Would you say a prayer for me?"

"Of course."

"Ask Him to witness me."

Krohe nodded and blessed the Excalibur blade with a splash of holy water.

****

Valdar reached into the holo tank and zoomed in toward one of the Crucible's many thorns. A single drone, Torni, worked feverishly on the last few incomplete sections of the immense gate.

His senior officers crowded around the tank along with three VIPs, a moniker Valdar disliked using for them, but it was apt.

"Torni? How much longer?" Valdar asked.

"I'll have the last of it down in the next few seconds. It'll take a few minutes to cure, then we're good to go."

"We'll have a short window of opportunity before the Xaros realize we're inside their network," Stacey said. "That door swings both ways, so once we get to Sletari, the probe within our Crucible will break the connection. We won't be able to come back through our gate unless we send an all clear through the probe we're bringing with us."

"This is what it was all for, wasn't it?" Valdar

looked at Stacey, then to the "Ranger" standing next to her. "The Xaros came through, wiped out the Earth, and almost finished the Crucible before we took it from them. All of that, and everything that followed, for one shot at their holy of holies."

"The Alliance would have brought a grand fleet for this moment." Stacey shook her head.

"I'll take a small force united in purpose over a giant mess of separate actors out for their own good," Valdar said, zooming the tank out to show the entire Crucible. Nearly a hundred human warships clustered around the supercarrier *Constantine* and the Dotok *Vorpral*. Two Ruhaald fleets filled up much of the rest of the jump gate's center. "Although...the Ruhaald aren't my first choice for allies."

"Needs must, Captain," Stacey said.

"Speaking of..." Valdar swiped a hand through the tank and a static model of Sletari came up. The Key Hole orbited the planet at a distance slightly farther than the moon from Earth. A different Crucible gate, more like the one over Ceres, held position over the alien world. A half-dozen holographic captains appeared around the tank.

"Task Force Gabriel," Valdar said, "we are the main effort for this operation. Once we're through the Crucible, we will make for best speed to the Key Hole. One of our mission specialists," Valdar said, looking at the disguised Ibarra, "will accompany the boarding party from the *Breitenfeld* and seize control of the target's command center. Once that is secure, the payload will go through final assembly and we will send it on to the Apex."

"Why the wait?" asked Captain Howser of the *Wyvern*. "Have the bomb ready before the gate to the Apex opens."

Valdar looked at the third VIP, Malal disguised as a lanky man in plain work overalls. Valdar hesitated, unsure if he wanted Malal to speak.

"It's a bomb that can destroy the galaxy," Stacey said. "Best not to arm it until we're absolutely sure the target is ready. The Little Boy atomic bomb dropped onto Hiroshima had its final assembly done on the way to the target...fun fact. In case anyone was interested."

"It cannot be stopped," Malal said. Stacey recoiled from him, startled by his words. "Activating the device will create the tear. The annihilation wave will form within minutes."

"Let me remind you all that the freighters *Nugget* and *Stugots* are carrying omnium that is a vital part of the bomb's payload," Valdar said. "We've rehearsed the void assembly, but those ships must be protected at all costs. Every other ship on this mission will do whatever it takes to get us to the Key Hole and then we must deliver the bomb. Failure is not an option."

A video feed from the ship's flight deck appeared in the holo tank. A drone flew through the force field and morphed into Torni. She looked up at the camera and gave a thumbs-up.

"Almost time," Valdar said. "Earth, all we've lost, all we might ever be, depends on this mission. *Gott Mit Uns*."

CHAPTER 13

The Engineer descended through bedrock, past striations marking geologic ages, and through the compacted remains of a city lost between continental forces. There, in a small void between the fault lines, a relic survived.

A ship formed into an elongated teardrop glowed in a cave, its bottom half buried in shattered stone.

The Engineer looked over the vessel, examining it down to the molecular level. A hand formed out of his clockwork shape and gently touched the ship's surface.

+What are you doing?+ Keeper sent from beyond the surface.

+The species that left this behind…their craftsmanship is superb, far greater than anything else we've encountered here. Wrought omnium. We spent centuries mastering the technique, then we abandoned the effort for photonics. Yet there is more here. I see the touch of many craftsmen, not all of the same race.+

+Why? No species that approached our glory could tolerate a peer competitor. No advanced species bothers with lesser beings.+

The Engineer marveled at his perfect reflection against the ship's hull.

+We were the first to walk the stars in our galaxy. We destroyed all other intelligences before they could ever pose a threat to us. If we had shepherded some of them along as slaves, perhaps they could have made some contribution to our civilization,+ the Engineer said.

+Heresy. Your time away from the Apex has affected your essence. None possess our purity or perfection. None will be allowed to sully our existence. The lower castes will shift through the ashes of this galaxy, then we will purge them from our ranks.+

+I admire your dogmatism.+ The Engineer felt a ripple through the fabric of space-time.

+That you even entertain other thoughts would put you up for censure. But we are both operating beyond our remit. I will forget this conversation ever happened.+

+Do you feel that?+ The Engineer left the ship and melded into the rock, returning to the surface quickly, like he was underwater and short on breath. The sensation grew stronger...emanating from one of the system's Crucible jump gates.

+Feel what?+

The Engineer broke through the surface and continued to space, toward the many-ringed jump gate leading to the Apex.

A Crucible gate over the once-inhabited world flared to life, and hundreds of ships poured through. Their design told of two different species acting in concert...with one oversized vessel boasting weapons of yet another race.

+Impossible!+ Keeper snapped across the void and took up residence within the center of the

Apex gate.

+Yet they are here. Secure the pathway to the Apex. That is your remit. I will deal with the intruders.+

+You must stop them. If the others even learn that this system was ever threatened...+

+I know the penalty. Do your job.+

The Engineer returned to Sletari. He summoned drones to defend the world and destroy the invaders. Their ships did not matter; only one specific passenger was of any significance. The Engineer took a position high over the world's North Pole, and waited for the rendezvous signal from Malal.

****

Valdar snapped out of his chair and went to the holo tank as telemetry data from the rest of the fleet flooded into it. The surface of Sletari reformed, updating from the Qa'Resh's millennia-old image. Malal and Ibarra were already at the tank, all looking intently at the Crucible gate the fleet had come through.

"The Xaros are realigning the gate," Stacey said. "We need to knock it off-line before almost every last drone in the galaxy comes through after us. Course, we break it too badly and we'll never get home."

"I don't have any plans for tomorrow," Valdar said. "Guns, mass rail cannon fire on a single point in the Crucible's structure and—"

"Wait..." Malal touched four firing points on the Crucible's shifting thorns. "Strike there. The damage will take the gate off-line for hours."

"Utrecht?"

"Helm pitch fourteen degrees to port after first volley," the gunnery officer called out.

White light flashed through the bridge as the rail cannons fired. Two of the points on the Crucible blinked red; the others followed suit soon after. All the Crucible's thorns froze in place.

"It will repair itself," Stacey said. She held up a hand and a tiny sliver of light glowed from her palm. "Our probe says it won't have a problem getting us back home, so long as we don't break that Crucible any more than we already have."

"Valdar?" Admiral Garret appeared in the holo tank. "We've got a problem."

Sletari grew in the tank. Hundreds of ruby threat icons appeared over the surface, all streaming toward a single point over a snow-covered patch of a mountain range. Valdar zoomed in; each icon was a single drone.

"We knew there'd be a Xaros garrison," Valdar said. "With all the firepower we've got, this should be a quick fight."

"Sletari is chicken feed compared to what's coming off the second moon," Garret said.

The holo zoomed over to a lush green planetoid surrounded by gigantic brass-colored rings. A Crucible gate, smaller than the one the allied fleet came through, was alive, spewing out drones and larger constructs.

"That wasn't in the Qa'Resh intelligence," Stacey said. "That's not supposed to be there!"

Course projections and an estimated time to contact traced away from the Xaros' active Crucible to the fleet. Valdar felt a cold pit form in his stomach.

"There's not enough time," he said. "I can't get to the Key Hole and deliver the bomb before we're up to our neck in drones."

"We didn't come all this way to quit now," Garret said. "Continue your mission. I'll hold them off as long as I can."

"The planet's defenses still function," Malal said.

"What are you talking about?" Valdar asked. "The Xaros would have wiped out every trace of the Mok'Tor when they conquered the planet."

"The Xaros preserve the remains of long-lost civilizations," Stacey said. Her doll face stared at Malal and Valdar swore he saw her gears turning.

"The Mok'Tor came to Sletari to plunder the remains of an older race, a race that slipped the bonds of mortality and left monuments to their glory for lesser beings to behold," Malal said.

"This is one of *your* planets," Valdar said.

"Correct." Malal reached into the tank and it zoomed in on the mountain range where the garrison drones massed. As the holo zoomed toward what

Valdar thought was a glacier, a city of tall crystalline spires and ivory bridges appeared. "Bring me here. I can access the world spirit and take control of the defenses."

Valdar pointed at Stacey. "Go. Get him to the flight deck."

CHAPTER 14

Hale grabbed a handle next to the Mule's ramp. Cortaro slapped him on the shoulder twice, telling him the ribbon-chute on his back was in place and ready to go.

The gauss cannons in the ship's defense turrets sent shivers through Hale's feet as they fired on Xaros drones.

"Landing zone is hot," Jorgen, the pilot, said through the Mule's IR. *"I can still make the drop but you'll have to vector in."*

"Give us a green light and we'll handle the rest." Hale looked over his shoulder at his Marines as they did final checks on each other's ribbon-chutes. Stacey and Malal stood toward the back of the compartment; neither had a ribbon-chute.

"Stacey, we can strap you to—"

"We've got it covered." She waved a hand at Hale.

The ramp lowered with a *thunk* and light flooded the Mule. Snowy mountain peaks swept past as Jorgen dipped the Mule lower. A blast of wind nudged Hale back as tiny flecks of snow and ice invaded the compartment.

"Air pressure nine thousand feet equivalent," Cortaro called out. "Winds ten knots north-northeast."

Hale tapped the information into his forearm screen and a bright green arrow appeared on his visor pointing toward the landing zone.

A warning horn sounded three times and a strobe light activated just above the lip of the open ramp.

"First one to make landfall drops the rendezvous beacon," Hale shouted over the gale winds. "After we form up, get Malal to the control room."

The horn and strobe light went steady.

"Jump! Jump! Jump!" Hale ran down the ramp and launched himself into the air. His world went almost silent as he fell, angling himself facedown.

The city lay a few miles up the valley. The crystalline spires looked as if they were carved from deep-blue ice mined out of ancient glaciers. The base of the city was bare rock—rock that tapered down to a column of stone that disappeared into a cloudbank hundreds of yards below.

Hale took his attention away from the impossible feat of engineering and twisted around. He counted each of his Marines in the air...but saw no sign of Stacey or Malal.

"Damn them. Chute! Parafoil!" His earpiece beeped twice as his ribbon-chute acknowledged his command. He slapped a palm against the release and the ribbon-chute unfolded into an arch shape. As it caught air, the risers snapped taut, sending a quake through his entire body. He looked up to check the canopy had formed correctly.

The flash of weapons fire crisscrossing the sky above and brief fireballs testified to the still-raging battle in the void. Hale steered himself toward the city, a tailwind buffeting him from side to side as it pushed him ahead.

Thank God for small favors, he thought as a shadow passed over him.

A Marine soared past Hale, his anti-grav lining propelling him forward faster than the wind.

"Standish? Is that you?"

"I'm going three for three as the first man on another planet, sir!"

Hale grit his teeth and angled toward the approaching lip of the city. A blast of wind slapped Hale aside and he struggled with his risers, fighting and failing to keep them untangled. Hale swung his legs back and managed to separate the carbon-fiber lines attaching him to his ribbon-chute. The wind relented and Hale twisted back toward the city, the distinct edge of which was closing fast.

A panicked cry for help came through the IR in a rush of static.

Hale found Standish hanging from his half-crumpled ribbon-chute and falling fast toward the city's edge.

"Standish! Dump your chute and go to your backup!"

The other Marine yanked at his risers...and descended beneath the plane of the city. Standish smacked into the bare rock. His parachute continued on and fell against the alabaster floor. Wind kept the canopy open, bouncing up and down.

Hale quickly guessed his rate of descent and the edge of the city.

"Chute! Ribbon!"

The parasail snapped up and morphed into a spiral. Hale fell faster, slowly angling toward Standish's flailing ribbon-chute.

Hale's boots slammed to the deck and he pulled the rings where the risers met his armor. The ribbon-chute slipped away on the breeze. He slid to a halt, grabbed Standish's ribbon-chute and heaved. He reeled the chute up...revealing ripped and frayed risers. He stopped, the lines tight and vibrating in resonance with the wind.

A *creak* came off the strained ribbon-chute and one of the lines snapped in Hale's hand. He snatched at the other but it broke just as he touched it. Hale leapt forward, grasping for the line as it snaked toward the edge.

"Standish!" The frayed edge slipped through his fingers and went over the edge.

Hale grabbed the white marble and looked down to the cloudy plain below.

An armored hand grabbed Hale by the wrist. Hale reared back and pulled Standish up and onto the city floor. Standish hugged the ground, his fingers trying to burrow into the marble.

"I like the ground," Standish said, his voice high and reedy. "Nice ground. Hard ground. No more fall." Standish tried to kiss the floor through his visor. "So pretty." Standish rubbed his hand against the marble from side to side.

"Standish, are you OK?"

Standish's head snapped up and looked at Hale as if he hadn't known he was there. He got to his feet and brushed himself off.

"Sir! Yes. Fine. Just fine. You're the first man on Sletari. Well done. Figured you deserved to win at least one."

"It's not a race, Standish. You're good to go?"

Standish winced and shifted the seat of his armor.

"Knew I should have hit the head before we left. I see the rest coming down toward the center. Shall we get moving and perhaps never mention this incident again?"

Hale drew his rifle off his shoulder and shook his head.

"Just get moving, Standish."

They ran toward the center of the city, past the base of a great tower so high its spire seemed to disappear in the sky. Smoother sections of the ground denoted roadways between the buildings, none of which had doors. Light refracted off the high bridges, casting golden geometric shapes that shifted with the wind.

"This place weirds me out, sir," Standish said. "Kind of like Malal's little hidey-hole."

"There's a reason for that." Hale stopped next to a tall square outcropping on a building and quickly peeked around the corner.

"Got you, sir," Cortaro said through Hale's helmet. *"You have Standish with you?"*

Hale ducked around the building and ran toward his Marines who were huddled within a garden of fern-like plants made of clear glass. Tiny motes of light moved up and down their veins.

Hale did a quick head count then asked, "Where's Stacey? Malal?"

Cortaro looked up and nodded.

A creature with bat-like wings and no head corkscrewed to the ground, holding Stacey in claws as thick as her arm. It let her go ten feet in the air and she shrieked and landed feetfirst. Her heels hit with a metallic clang and the rest of her flopped to the ground. Her head struck a low bench, knocking an alabaster chunk loose with the impact.

Hale ran to her and reached out to help her up, but pulled his hand back at the last instant.

Stacey looked up, a puff of chalk over her forehead. When she looked at him with those still eyes, Hale felt a pang of guilt.

"I'm fine." She got up and rubbed her arm across her head. "I'm rather durable like this."

"Sorry." Hale inched away from her as a chill crept into his armor.

The bat creature landed gracefully a few yards away and folded its wings to the ground. Its surface shimmered and then the wings drew inward. It morphed into a human form with all the detail of a blank mannequin.

Malal tilted his head back, then twisted it from side to side.

"It has been too long," he said. "Just as I remembered it. The sky is different. The old constellations are gone, lost to the dance."

"Malal." Stacey snapped her fingers at him. "People are dying to buy us the time you need to reactivate the defenses, not feel nostalgic."

"We're not far." Malal walked off, his limbs lengthening to a pace Hale matched with a jog.

"Watch the skies," Steuben said. "The Eagles pulled the drones away but they may return."

Hale fell in just behind Stacey and Malal. His heart skipped a beat each time an odd reflection caught on the bridges and buildings polished to a mirror sheen.

"Malal, why did you build this city on that rock column?" Stacey asked. "Doesn't seem like a place to build something you want to last."

"We didn't." Malal looked at her, his face elongated and his eye sockets bulging out ever so slightly. "The city did not move. The mountains did."

"But that kind of erosion, a shift in tectonic plates...it would take millions of years," she said.

"This was a place of rest, repose. A pause from the archologies and the great task." Malal slowed and veered toward a building, a pyramid with the upper third missing. "I amused myself with the natives, mammals much like you. I harvested them all to prolong *her* life. When *she* saw what could be done with the technique, *she* used my knowledge, my work, to open the door. And when it came time to claim my reward, *she* slammed it in my face."

"Malal..." Stacey said with a warning tone.

"What's he talking about?" Hale asked.

"Nothing that matters to us," she said.

"Malal, did this *she* of yours leave any defenses?" Standish asked. "Valuable stuff tends to have alarms. Guard dogs. That kind of thing."

Malal sauntered up to the side of the incomplete pyramid and waved a hand across the surface. A golden three-dimensional lattice appeared in his hand's wake. Segments of the lattice jumped from node to node without any pattern. Hale felt like he was looking at a screen from a dead television channel.

"There is no need for guards if no one can find the door," Malal said.

The longer Hale looked at the pyramid, shapes formed in the ivory wall. Aliens with the elongated heads and bulbous eyes close to those Malal displayed earlier walked across the wall, their outlines bright like the afterglow of a sharp light across his eyes. Behind each of the aliens, a diminutive form followed, a half dome shape with long arms dangling beneath. Crystal plates caught against the light.

"Stacey...are those..."

"Not now," she said.

"Contact!" Yarrow pointed his rifle up and over the pyramid. Four Xaros drones whipped around a building and sped straight toward the Marines.

"Egan, Q-shell." Cortaro switched the selector switch on his own rifle to HIGH power and took aim.

Hale took cover next to the pyramid. The IR channel to Durand and her fighters had a poor connection, but it was something.

"Gall, this is Roughneck Six. Hostiles inbound, we're in the open and need air support."

All he got was static.

"Gall, Roughneck Six, how copy?"

Egan's rifle snapped as he fired the quadrium shell. A streak of silver zipped toward the first batch of incoming drones and exploded into sky-blue bolts of lightning. The energy arced from drone to drone, knocking them off-line and sending them into free fall. The Marines opened up, shattering all but one of the drones before they hit the ground. The survivor crashed into a small grove of trees, shattering them with a crack of breaking glass.

"More!" Standish shouted. "Five o'clock."

Hale aimed his rifle at the mass of jagged trees and swirling dust and saw no trace of the drone.

"Rough...come in!" Durand said through the IR.

"Gall, this is—"

A pair of ruby lights rose from the broken

trees. Hale snapped off a shot that hit the ground just in front of the lights, sending up a shower of dirt and grass. A red disintegration beam slashed out and struck the pyramid just over Hale's head. He rolled to the side and banged off another shot into the fog of soil and pulverized trees.

A beam clipped his thigh. The aegis armor resisted the beam's effects, but the glancing blow felt like someone had slapped his leg with a hot poker. He lurched over and fell against the pyramid, his leg twitching of its own accord.

The lights in the fog bounced around as his Marines inundated the area with gauss shots. A ruby beam struck the ground a few yards away and cut a line through the ground straight for him.

The pyramid holding him up vanished and Hale felt something jerk him aside. He landed face down on a floor made up of interlocking starburst tiles, each seemingly alive with tiny gold lights across its surface. He looked up and saw Stacey's booted feet.

"This isn't meant for him," Malal said.

Hale got up and swept his rifle back to the

direction he'd fallen from. He was inside the pyramid, but the interior was impossibly big, much larger than the volume of the structure he'd seen outside. The inner walls were matte white, extending up to a bright point of light at the apex of the pyramid. Crystals the size of footballs floated motionless in the air along the walls. There was a single opening the size of a garage door. Hale saw his Marines locked in combat with drones, but there was no sound of the battle.

Hale reached out to the doorway and his fingers stopped against an invisible wall.

"Let me out! I need to help them," Hale said to Malal.

"This isn't meant for him," Malal said from just behind Hale.

"Then open the door so I can—" Hale froze as Malal pressed a thumb against the Marine's forehead. Hale's mouth stayed open mid-sentence.

"What did you do?" Stacey asked.

"I have no time for him. He will remain there while we get what we came for." Malal turned around and walked toward a dais in the middle of the pyramid. A churning column of light extended up from the floor to the point of light high above.

"This is just like your vault," Stacey said, "the one where we got the codex."

"It should be. I built them both." Malal stopped a few feet from the wide column. Wisps formed near the surface, like fish clustering around the side of a tank when feeding time neared. "Hello, my pretties. Did you miss me?"

Ghostly faces formed in the column, mouths opened in terror, and the wisps fled away.

"The defenses, Malal, turn them on before the fleet is destroyed," Stacey said.

"What of my other purpose?"

"Get the code to destroy the drones *after* the battle is over." Stacey pointed back to the doorway. "Hurry! They're dying out there!"

"It's time for you to meet someone." Malal pressed a hand to the column and a pulse of light shot up the column and through the tip of the pyramid.

"What are you talking about?" Stacey's hand crept toward the kill switch on her belt. A single press of a button and the governor in Malal's chest would render him down to a rapidly expanding mess of subatomic particles.

The ancient being's hand snaked out and caught her by the wrist.

"None of that." Malal yanked her off her feet and dragged her toward him. His arms coiled around her, binding Stacey from her shoulders to her ankles.

"Stop this! You'll never get what want. We had a bargain, damn you!"

"I made a better one." Malal pulled her away as a searing light descended the column and resolved into interlocking gears nearly half the width of the pyramid.

Stacey struggled weakly. She tried to turn her head away from the apparition, but it pressed against her mind, its image burned against her closed eyes.

"This is the Engineer," Malal said to her. "Beautiful, isn't it?"

"Don't do this…" she said quietly.

"It is already done." Malal leaned back to gaze upon the Engineer. "Here it is," he shouted. "This one knows where the ascension gate is hidden. I know how to open it. Take her mind and together we will find eternity."

The Engineer's gears shifted inside out.

"Come forward," Malal said. "Do not fear this one. She is a mockery of immortality, a weak servant to her betters. Come and claim her."

The Engineer's form contracted, morphing into deep-green armor over a photonic body nearly twenty feet tall.

Terror coursed through her as the Engineer raised a hand, light swirling in its palm.

+Release me,+ Malal sent to her. His grip on her arms and hands loosened, allowing her to grasp the kill switch. +Release me before it realizes the mistake it made.+

Light burned through cracks in the Engineer's armor as it reached for her.

Stacey tapped a code into the kill switch. Malal flung her aside as the governor, a sphere of bent hoops, fell out of his chest. Malal's hands morphed into blades and he rammed them both into the Engineer's chest. Raw light spilled from the wounds as a squeal rose in the air.

Malal grew larger. Golden light coursed up his arms as he slid his blades deeper.

"Greed and impatience are poor qualities for a god." Malal cracked the Engineer's chest open and slammed the Xaros lord to the ground. Malal raised a blade and morphed it into a wicked claw that he plunged into a gap in the armor.

The Engineer thrashed wildly, breaking the tile floor with each hit. Malal withdrew a glowing orb from the armor. Light seeped out of the Engineer's husk and into the ball. The armor collapsed to nothing but a mesh and a few plates, empty.

Malal held the Engineer's essence up to the sky.

"Such potential...wasted!" Malal crushed the globe between his fingers and light oozed down his arm. Malal absorbed the light, then tossed a few shards of glass back to the deflated armor.

He picked up the governor and pressed it back into his chest, then went to the column of mottled light.

"What was that, Malal?" Stacey was on her side, her eyes glued to the Engineer's remnants.

"You want the code to stop the drones. The Engineer had it. I can give it to you soon. I must digest all he has to offer." Malal raised his hands and the golden lattices appeared. "Now to end the problem of the Xaros reinforcements."

"You used me as bait!"

"You wanted the code. I told you this is where we would find it. What is the problem?"

"Why didn't you let me in on this little plan of yours? You think I wanted to have my mind almost drained out by that-that-that…" she pointed a shaky finger at the Engineer's remains.

"Raw emotion cannot be faked. If you knew the plan, the Engineer would have felt it in your aura. Your fear lured him in."

"How did you know I wouldn't hit your kill switch when you gave me the chance?"

"You chose to survive beyond the limits of your flesh and blood. I knew what you would do given the choice between killing me and dying at the Engineer's hand, or trusting me with the chance to live."

"I didn't choose this." Stacey tapped her fingers against her cold metal chest.

"Then return to your old body."

"I will die in seconds if that—" Stacey snapped her mouth shut. A very small moment of clarity touched her mind, and she understood what Malal was getting at. Her body was nigh-immortal. It could last for thousands on top of thousands of years, and she would rather live on like this than embrace the end.

She looked from Hale to Malal and realized that she had moved beyond the humanity of her birth. What Malal wanted out of his bargain with her and the Qa'Resh made a great deal more sense, even if the price still horrified her.

"Many of the other cities have fallen to time," Malal said. "The world spirit is weak, but still useful." The golden lattices faded away.

"That one doesn't need to know." Malal walked toward Hale. He waved a hand toward the Engineer's armor and it began to burn away like a destroyed drone. His omnium body glowed slightly from within, dampening the surrounding shadows. "I dislike this one. He possesses a conscience that may interfere with our task."

"That is why I care for him so much," she

said. "He is a good man. Not like you. Not like my grandfather…and not like me. Not anymore."

"Prattle." Malal swiped a thumb across Hale's forehead as he walked to the door.

"—get out there and…what happened?" Hale pointed at the clear door where Orozco and Egan tapped at the outer wall. The rest of the Marines formed a perimeter around the door.

Malal stopped across from Egan and waited for the Marine to knock on the wall again. Egan's hand went forward and bounced off Malal's face.

The Marine reared back, raising his rifle.

"Jiminy Fricking Christmas!" Egan angled his muzzle away from Malal.

"Told you there was a door here." Orozco glanced around Malal. "Captain and the VIP are both here."

"Give me an update." Hale stopped over the threshold. He ducked his head outside to gauge the size of the pyramid, then leaned back inside and confirmed that it really was bigger within.

"Took care of the drones," Cortaro said, "no injuries. *Breitenfeld*'s been calling. I tried to tell them you three vanished inside a pyramid and we were trying to find you. Valdar didn't seem too upset with that answer. Guess we've had stranger things happen."

Malal pointed a finger at the distant moon hosting the Xaros-controlled Crucible. Hale made out a burning point of light within the crown of thorns.

A hum filled his ears. Hale tapped his helmet, but the sound wasn't from his earpiece. A bow of green light formed across the sky, stretching from one horizon to the other. Bronze-colored lightning snapped across the bow.

"How I missed this," Malal said.

A ray of green light erupted from the bow and shot straight at the Xaros Crucible. The ends of the bow retreated to the base of the ray as it cut across space to the moon. The ray blasted through the moon's artificial rings and struck the surface almost dead center. Fissures broke across the surface…then the moon exploded with a flash of light. Fragments the size of mountains went spinning through space, obliterating the Xaros Crucible within seconds.

Hale's jaw dropped open as the broken moon

slowly spread across the sky.

"Hey, Malal," Standish said, waving to the entity, "how about a couple of those for Earth? Sure would make defending the planet easier if we have a nice big Death Ray button to push."

"Can I rip his tongue out?" Malal asked Stacey.

"No." Stacey looked across the sky. Flashes from the raging void battle continued. "The Xaros reinforcements are cut off but we still have to deal with whatever got away from the gate. What else can you do?"

"The planet is drained. Let us move on to the gate you call the Key Hole," Malal said.

"Hale, you heard him." Stacey looked up at the celestial carnage. "All that's going to come down here. We'll see the first fragments in the atmosphere in hours. The entire planet will be a meteor-blasted wasteland in days. Hale?"

The captain had his head cocked up, staring at the destruction.

She slapped him on the shoulder.

"Yes! Calling evac." Hale lowered his head

and mumbled into an IR channel.

CHAPTER 15

Keeper watched as Sletari's second moon broke apart. His essence stirred within the center of the Key Hole as he tried to control the remaining Crucible. It remained off-line, bent on repairing itself.

+Engineer. Where are you? We need a conduit to the rest of our drones. We are trapped without it.+

Keeper stretched out to Sletari...and couldn't find his peer's presence.

+Engineer?+

Keeper's form contracted into a rapidly spinning neutron star. The humans and their allies stood on the threshold to the Apex with a massive fleet. They'd blocked or destroyed the only connections to the galaxy-spanning jump-gate network…and they must have killed the Engineer.

A sensation spread through Keeper's being, an old, atavistic reaction that served the Xaros when they were primitives. A feeling not experienced since the annihilation wave began its inexorable march across their home galaxy.

Fear.

Keeper had already sent a distress signal through the Crucible network when the humans first arrived. The drones would swarm toward Sletari once they realized the jump gates in the system were off-line…but it would take months for the first reinforcements to arrive.

The drone armada that survived the destruction of the moon was large, capable of defeating the invaders. Keeper's algorithms put his forces chance of victory well above seventy percent, but the humans had proved too nimble and adept for him to trust the odds. He scanned the human fleet and found a discrepancy beyond the Earth's ship's normal composition.

Two freighters full of omnium…and a second

jump-engine signature within the *Breitenfeld*, a ship encountered by the Xaros far too many times. Keeper grasped his enemy's plan after a few seconds of denial. They hadn't come just to destroy the Key Hole…they were here for the Apex.

+I have a purpose.+ Keeper turned his attention to the jump gate leading back to the ark carrying all that remained of the Xaros. He was entrusted with the care of the Apex; his remit to shepherd his race across the intergalactic void was absolute. Any threat to the Apex meant he was a failure, and the Xaros did not tolerate failure.

There was only one way to reach the Apex. Keeper reached into the Key Hole's command system and prepared the self-destruct protocols. He would destroy the humans' only chance at striking at the heart of the Xaros, then he would flee to a neighboring star with a Crucible, persecute the war against the vermin infesting the galaxy, and rebuild a new Key Hole. It would be centuries before the Apex arrived. The others would not care how the galaxy was won, only that they arrived whole and to a sea of stars cleansed of all other intelligent life.

Keeper activated the self-destruct sequence…and nothing happened.

It felt the fabric of space-time shift as a wormhole formed almost on top of him.

+No! I have the situation under control. I can fix this!+

A midnight-blue claw reached out of the wormhole and snatched Keeper out of the void. Keeper sent his drones one final command before the claw snapped back into the wormhole.

****

Valdar clung to his holo tank as the *Breitenfeld* tilted onto her side.

"Number two battery, fire!" Valdar called out. The bridge shook as the rail cannons loosed another volley. In the holo tank, tiny red arrows extended away from his ship toward a Xaros battle-cruiser analog that had broken through the Ruhaald lines on a course toward the *Breitenfeld*.

Ruhaald fighters swarmed over the Xaros

229

ship, destroying point defense positions as they spouted over the ship's surface. Valdar watched as a dozen Ruhaald craft vanished off the holo tank, replaced with red X's as the rail cannon shells closed the distance.

Valdar's hands gripped tighter as the munitions closed…and one broke through the enemy's defenses. The Xaros ship bucked like it had been kicked, its fore angled away from the rest of the craft, her keel broken. The Ruhaald fighters circled around to the breach in the ship's hull and inundated the crater with fire. Cracks broke across the hull as it burned away from within.

"We're still not even, Jarilla," Valdar said under his breath.

"Drones in sector twelve!" Ericson called out.

"Clear them out." Valdar swiped through the holo tank. His task force remained on course to the Key Hole, separated from the battling armadas. The alien structure loomed ahead, hundreds of miles in diameter.

"Flight deck, this is the captain." Valdar held a finger between his ship and the Key Hole and nodded as the estimated time of flight between his ship and the innermost ring of the jump gate appeared. "Prepare to launch boarding party soon as we've dealt with these drones."

"Valdar..." Ibarra came up in a window. He was in one of the combat-loaded Mules in the hangar and wore Ranger armor but carried no weapon. Having gotten used to the idea of the man as a ghost, Valdar still had trouble accepting that Ibarra finally walked amongst the living. "Our Qa'Resh probe tells me the Key Hole just activated. Very strange readings, nothing it's ever seen before."

"Is there something I'm supposed to do about it?" Valdar asked.

One of the forward windows cracked as a Xaros stalk tip broke through the blast plates. As the drone ripped the shutter away like it was opening a tin can, the bridge broke out in shouted warnings and a pair of Marines put themselves between the captain and the threat.

The drone exploded into burning fragments as gauss shells thumped against the bridge's armor.

"I got it," Durand said. *"Everyone OK in there?"*

"We appreciate your judicious aim," Valdar said. "Ibarra, can you and that probe of yours get the job done or not?"

"We'll see when we get into the command center. Torni is waiting for Malal to start work on the detonator. Are they back yet?"

A blinking icon appeared behind the *Breitenfeld*, the Mule he'd sent to Sletari's surface with a pair of Eagle fighters escorting it.

"They'll land soon. Launch the boarding party. We'll have Malal's bomb put together as soon as we can," Valdar said.

"Sir, something's happening." Ericson zoomed the tank out. The Xaros pulled away from the allied armada, and a swarm of drones formed a screen over the main force. As quadrium shells slammed against the screen, light crackled across the curtain of drones like static. Rail cannons shredded entire swathes of drones with fragmenting shells, but a gap never appeared in the screen.

"What are they doing?" she asked.

"I have a feeling we're about to find out." Valdar tapped a screen and opened a new channel.

"*Nugget, Stugots*, engage docking maneuvers and prep the omnium for the trigger. Slave your control systems to my conn and abandon ship once the bomb is complete."

"Incoming!" Ericson shouted.

Five silver lances, each half the size of the *Breitenfeld*, burst through the Xaros drones. Hundreds of drones broke apart as the lances bulldozed right through them. They sped toward a cluster of Ruhaald cruisers.

The line of human and Ruhaald ships opened fire, and bright specks of light from rail cannons and Ruhaald energy blasts spat toward the lances. The Xaros weapons changed their flight path…angling toward the *Breitenfeld* and dodging every shot sent against them.

Valdar watched as the lances' trajectory plots stabilized…and his heart skipped a beat.

"*Nugget, Stugots*, break off docking and take evasive maneuvers, now!"

"What about us, sir?" Geller asked.

"Hold steady. Guns, load quadrium shells and set a wide dispersion pattern."

Utrecht nodded and tapped madly. "Q-shells won't stop those things, sir."

"It'll stop them from changing course. Easier to hit." He opened a new channel. "Task Force Gabriel, protect the omnium haulers at all cost. *Manticore* destroyers, there is no fight after this. Burn out your crystals if you have to."

"Firing!" Utrecht announced.

The q-shells raced to intercept. The lances angled to one side, their path now missing two of the three shells.

"Utrecht…"

"We're working up the new firing solution."

The three shells ignited, casting webs of electric filament into the void. One tendril latched onto a lance and arced to two more. The affected Xaros weapons stopped accelerating and went tumbling end over end.

"Guns, another volley of q-shells. All ships, open fire!"

The *Manticore*-class ships twisted toward the incoming projectiles and opened fire. A wave of energy blasts streaked away from the Task Force like sparks off a welding arc. The ship shook again as the batteries sent up another q-shell volley.

The two active lances jinked from side to side, maneuvers that would have turned his crew into pulp if his ship tried the same thing.

"Load canister shells and fire at will," Valdar said.

Two of the disabled lances took hits from energy cannons and burned away. A gauss cannon shot off the forward anti-air turrets nicked one of the Xaros weapons screaming toward the *Nugget*. It bounced to the side and into a hail of energy bolts.

Valdar looked through the rip in the front blast shields and saw a glint of silver against the void.

"Slew to two-seven mark nine and fire!" Utrecht said.

The recoil sent Valdar into the side of the holo tank. He looked up, praying the lance had taken a hit…and saw it streak across his bow.

"*Nugget*! Abandon ship! That is a direct—"

The lance slammed into the *Nugget*, ripping it in half. Glowing omnium cubes spilled into the void. The lance kept moving and embedded against the

Stugots. The impact sent the conjoined pair spinning around.

"Guns," said Valdar, slamming a fist against the holo tank, "target the *Stugots*. The Xaros used this tactic against Eighth Fleet. That lance will break into drones if we don't destroy it now."

"But the *Stugots*, the crew..." Utrecht said.

Valdar zoomed toward the *Stugots* and saw the lance slide into the ship's hull. Sparks of ruby light flashed through portholes and from within the bridge.

"They're already dead. Do it."

"Valdar, Ibarra here. We're in the Key Hole's command dome. Ben says he can have a wormhole to the Apex in a few more minutes." Ibarra's transmission came up as a voice wave within the tank.

Valdar bit his lip, unsure how exactly to convey that their mission was a failure.

"More lances!" Ericson said. "Eight more, all vectoring right for us."

Valdar looked over his video screens. On the flight deck, Torni and Malal huddled around the jump engine from the Ruhaald. He came up with a solution—a long shot—but still a solution.

"Conn, all ahead full, take us into the Key Hole. Torni, can you hear me?" Valdar asked.

"Sir?" She looked up from the bomb to the camera.

"Can you ignite the weapon without the omnium supply?"

"No, we need a significant amount of energy to begin the cascade—"

"What about the *Breitenfeld*'s jump engine? She's got a full charge in her dark-energy batteries. Can you do it with that?"

A hush fell across the bridge. The crew looked up from their workstations to their captain.

Torni nodded slowly. "I can do that for you, sir." She looked at Malal quickly then said, "But if you can get us to the Apex, we might—"

"Get to the engine room and do what you have to. I'm taking us through the Key Hole. We came here to destroy the Apex, no other reason." He cut the transmission. "Conn?"

"Aye aye, course laid. Full speed ahead."

Valdar opened a ship-wide channel. "Crew of the *Breitenfeld*, this is Valdar. Our chance to destroy the Xaros threat once and for all is almost lost. We have one chance left—to take our ship through the Key Hole. There, we will turn our own ship into the instrument of their destruction. We won't come back, but we will pay the price to ensure that Earth—all of humanity—has a future. I will remain on the bridge. All nonessential personnel are permitted to abandon ship."

Silence reigned for a few seconds, then the bridge crew turned back to their stations. The normal chatter of a ship in the middle of a battle returned.

"We're with you all the way, sir," Ericson said. "Have been since the moment you first came aboard."

Valdar gave her a half smile.

"Ibarra, this is Valdar. Need you to open a wormhole for my ship to the Apex. We'll be there in three minutes."

"Ben, can you do that? Just the one ship? Better than nothing. Hey, unhand me you knuckle-dragging oafs!...Valdar! Tell these Rangers to let me go! Because I have *to be with the ship when she goes through...I finally have my own two feet and I will use them to walk on my own, thank*

you very much…Isaac, did you catch any of that? Your wormhole is waiting, but we can get your ship through only if your jump engine…I'll explain it when I get there. Ben will stay behind, keep the door open for us to come back. If we're that lucky."

"I monitored. Get in your Mule. We'll do a scoop landing on our way through. Torni?"

"At the jump engine. It will take us at least an hour to prep the Breit*'s engine. If you can get me and the bomb to a high-energy mass in the Apex, we can pull the trigger a lot faster."*

"Prep for the worst-case scenario. We need to be ready, not hopeful."

"I've seen the inside of the Apex, sir. We might have an option."

"Get to it." Valdar swiped a finger across a control panel and called up an overlay with all the active escape pods. All present.

"I hope this is the right call," he said. *"Gott Mit Uns."*

The *Breitenfeld* neared the center of the Key Hole, and a white-hot portal opened before the ship.

CHAPTER 16

Keeper fell through the abyss, his form reduced to the Xaros' base humanoid shape. Arms and legs flailed as air rushed around him. A plain of volcanic rock appeared, riven by thin streaks of magma. He slowed, then came to a stop gently on his feet. The sensation of ground against his skin, something he hadn't experienced in eons, appalled him.

To be forced back into his pre-exalted shape was humiliating.

The ground morphed into overlapping disks of roiling omnium as a circle of thrones rose around him, each ornately beautiful and distinct from the others. The sky shifted to the constellations once visible above the Xaros' annihilated home world.

One throne grew taller and wider than the others, the backing covered in small spikes of shimmering jewels that mimicked the mountain range where the most powerful Xaros once called home.

The now familiar sensation of fear coursed through Keeper.

Red smoke seeped from the thrones and coalesced into Xaros, all much larger than Keeper. Three yellow eyes opened on each of their faces, all boring into Keeper.

The Xaros on the high throne arrived last. Scaled armor covered his body, each half-moon shape holding a star cluster within, denoting property from his holdings that once spanned a galaxy. There was only one way to greet the High King. Keeper fell to his knees and bared his throat.

+Keeper…we are disappointed,+ the High King said.

+We expected the General to try to destroy the gate from our Apex to our new home,+ one of the other Masters said. +We prepared for his betrayal. Imagine our surprise when it came from you.+

+Where is the General?+ The High King leaned forward, his third eye ablaze.

+Lost!+ Keeper backpedaled, but froze as the High King's telekinetic grip snarled around him. +He failed in his task to cleanse the galaxy of pollution, died at the hands of a race called—+

An invisible tendril wrapped around Keeper's throat, loosening only to let him breathe every so often.

+A Xaros destroyed by a vermin,+ a Master said. +Never, not even in the early days of our righteous annexation of our galaxy, did one of our own fall to our inferiors. We chose this galaxy because there was no threat to ourselves. A galaxy of fertile worlds for us to take, a laboratory for us to find the ultimate answer at our leisure. Now Keeper tells us that a credible threat exists to us...to our goal.+

+The risk is unacceptable,+ said another Master on the other side of the circle. +Let us carry on to another galaxy. Another may carry the dishonorable mantle of General, one more competent.+

+Impossible,+ said the High King as he

dropped Keeper to the ground. +The star at the core of the Apex is failing. It cannot carry us any farther than this galaxy. Where is the Engineer? He will answer for this.+

+The Engineer...+ Keeper lowered his head. +The Engineer was also destroyed by the humans.+

The High King raised a fist and slammed it against his throne, shattering an armrest into a million splinters. The other Masters remained silent. The High King flicked a fingertip at Keeper and his memories raced through his mind, from the moment the General awakened him until now.

+What was your remit, Keeper?" the High King asked.

+To safeguard the Apex during our passage through the long night. To ensure the galaxy was ready for our glorious arrival. But this is not my fault! The General was weak...foolish! The Engineer knew his creation was flawed. Together, he and I sought out a—"

The High King flashed a palm at Keeper, silencing him.

+You conspired with the General and the

Engineer to hide their failure. Then you used forbidden technology—wormholes!—to carry out your remit,+ the High King said.

The Masters hissed at Keeper. Some twisted their hands into arcane symbols to ward off the shame of Keeper's actions.

+The wormholes destroyed our home,+ said the High King, settling back into his throne. +They set off the annihilation wave that drove us to the void and interrupted our great works. Then you risked their use in our new home…knowing full well that our Apex could not survive another journey if another such disaster occurred.+

His eyes blazed brighter.

+You risked my existence to cover for your failure.+ The High King lifted a finger slightly.

A plinth rose in front of Keeper. A small shard of midnight-colored glass floated on top. Keeper saw his reflection in the glass…and his impending doom.

+The possibility of such a disaster was miniscule.+ Keeper looked to one of the Masters, his old patron, and knelt at his feet. +The vermin were using such devices, crude tools with a much higher risk. We had to act quickly before they created an annihilation wave.+

+We were not consulted.+ His old patron kicked Keeper away.

+Keeper thinks himself wiser than us,+ another Master said. +Now the vermin are at our doorstep. Give him the blade!+

+The blade!+ sounded from the circle.

+No! Wait!+ Keeper gripped the floor as an invisible force dragged him by the feet toward the plinth and the instrument of his destruction. +The vermin are weak. We destroyed their only source of unity and now they war amongst themselves. Our victory is within reach. I haven't failed. I haven't failed!+

+Yes, you have.+ The High King glanced up. There, high over the council, the *Breitenfeld* emerged from a Crucible ring.

Keeper ceased his struggle. He grabbed the blade out of the air and held the tip to his breast. The blade burned like acid, eroding his hand away.

+May my memory survive.+ Keeper thrust

the blade into his chest. He screamed as the weapon broke down his photonic matrix, tearing his soul into worthless scrap that dissipated into nothing. A small pile of dust from Keeper's shell remained.

The High King scattered the remnants with a thought.

+Such is the price of failure.+ One hand dug into his remaining armrest, cracking the wrought crystal as his gaze bore into the distant *Breitenfeld*.

+I will put an end to this myself.+

****

Valdar stared out from his bridge, his mouth slightly agape at the impossible sight beyond. A blue-white spike stretched out beneath his ship and ran to a pale star in the distance. Jade-green mountains covered the interior of the Apex. Valdar squeezed his eyes shut for a moment, trying to comprehend the scale of what he saw.

"Wow," Ensign Geller said, gripping the side of his chair as if afraid of falling off.

"Am I the only one that thought we'd show

up *outside* this thing?" Ericson asked.

"Helm," said Valdar. When Geller didn't answer, Valdar slapped his palm against the side of his chair.

"Sir?" Geller snapped out of his shock.

"Attitude control. Radiation. What's going on out there?"

Geller spun his chair around and looked over his station. "No gravity pulling on us, not even from that star. Hull temperature is near absolute zero…which doesn't make any sense as we're in direct starlight. But we're inside something the size of…that can't be right."

"Spit it out."

"We're as far from that star as Mars is from the sun. That spike running beneath us is…as wide as Jupiter? No. Can't be."

"Fly your instruments, not what you can see. How far are we from the spike?"

"Laser sounding puts us at a little over four hundred kilometers," Utrecht answered.

"Captain, engine room," Commander Levin said through the IR, *"the jump engine is acting a mite peculiar.*

She's showing an open wormhole, but there's no power going through the batteries."

"Yes, about that," Ibarra said as he joined the conversation, *"Ben's got the door to the Key Hole jammed open just enough for us to get back. If we could hurry up and get that bomb set before we become permanent residents…that would be great."*

"Torni?"

"I'm on my way back to the flight deck," Torni said, *"again. Our jump engine is not—I repeat not—ready to blow up. Malal had almost finished. He vanished when we came through. Do you know where he went?"*

"Ibarra?"

"I guess Malal opted out of a one-way trip. I can't reach Stacey. She must be with him."

"I don't need him to finish the bomb on the flight deck or to rig our jump engine, but I can't be in two places at once," Torni said.

"What do you need to set off the bomb? I don't see any giant piles of omnium lying around."

"We were going to attach it to the outer hull. Get me down to that spike. It should do the trick."

"XO, send a shore party down via drop pods.

Torni will catch up once the area's secure."

"Aye aye." Ericson put a hand to her earpiece and began issuing orders.

Valdar looked out to the star, and the sense of just how small and insignificant he and his ship were compared to the Apex finally hit home. They were a speck, a mote of dust against an elephant's hide, yet he had a very distinct feeling that their arrival had been noticed.

CHAPTER 17

Hale readied his rifle as the drop pod door raised up. The blue-white spike spread like an infinite plain, the edge lost to a distant haze.

Standish leaned out the door beside Hale. He reached a toe toward the surface, like he was testing the water of a pool.

"Really?" Hale asked.

"Just because the drop pods are stable doesn't mean—hey!" Standish lurched out the door, propelled by a solid kick from Bailey. Ripples of golden light spread from each of the Marine's footfalls. Standish stopped, then jumped up and down slightly. He gave a thumbs-up to Hale and ran to the side of another drop pod and took cover against a landing strut.

Hale jumped out and swept around the drop pod. There was nothing but the spike and a pale blue haze clinging to the surface. He made out the star at the center of the Apex. Above, the jade-green interior twinkled with golden stars.

The drop pods formed a rough circle on the spike. Heat seeped through Hale's leg from the retro-thrusters on a pod. Looking at the ground beneath the pod, he saw it was as pristine as the rest of the spike floor. The thrusters were known to ignite forest fires and boil soil into glass during landings. For there to be no effect on the spike...

Thumps rippled through the ground as Elias hurried over.

"Hell of a place to set down," the armor said. "No cover. No concealment. Everything with eyes saw our pods burn in."

"Those green mountains on the shell? It would take the *Breitenfeld* days to get there. Maybe it'll take the Xaros that long to get out here," Hale said.

A horn blared in the distance. A wave of silver light broke from the base of the spike and slowly rippled through the jade mountains, leaving a dense pattern of light in its wake. Hale watched the wave propagate outward…until it collided with an identical wave coming from the opposite direction.

"I shouldn't have said that." Hale tightened his hold on his rifle.

"You shouldn't have said that." Elias tapped a heel against the spike. "I can't get my anchor through this. Our rail guns will have only one shot a piece."

"Wait…without your anchor, the recoil will send you flying."

"Like I said. One shot."

"Sir, we've got atmo," Yarrow said from the other side of the drop pod. "Composition matches what we've found inside the Crucible. Permission to crack?" The corpsman gripped the bottom of his visor at Hale's nod. He lifted it briefly and let the air flow over his face. He took a shallow breath, then lifted his visor all the way and breathed normally.

"It's like…fresh mountain air. Bit thin." Yarrow's breath steamed out of his mouth.

Video feeds from each drop pod fed into Hale's helmet, each showing a nearly identical picture of the landscape around them. His Marines and six other armor soldiers clustered around the drop pods for cover.

Colonel Carius strode into the center of the loose perimeter and held up an IR beacon. The low roar of a Mule's engines broke through the air. Hale caught sight of the ship's thruster flames in the haze, between him and the barely visible *Breitenfeld* high above.

Bailey rapped her knuckles against Bodel's leg.

"Help me up, mate," she said, gesturing with her chin to the top of a drop pod. Bodel bent his hand into a scoop for Bailey to sit in and set her onto the higher vantage point. She assembled her rail rifle and wiggled into a prone firing position, spare battery packs set to her side.

"Any better up there?" Egan asked.

Bailey pressed her eye against her scope.

"I can see exactly two things up here—jack and shit. Least I can cover the whole perimeter from up here," she said.

Hale tapped his fingertips against his rifle.

"Elias, guess you don't have an issue with

253

tight spaces. What about...really god damn wide spaces?" Hale asked.

"I once spent three weeks on an asteroid over-watch position waiting for a Chinese military intelligence ship to come through. Lot of time looking out into the void. Knowing you're at the center of the infinite makes it easier. Here...this is wrong. We see the wall and we think we're in a covered stadium. Your mind is trying to rationalize the impossible. Stop it."

Hale's mouth went dry. "How the hell could they even build this thing? I mean—I mean..."

Elias reached down and gently set his armored hand against Hale's shoulder.

"Your crunchies are going through the same thing. Why don't you and Cortaro go check the perimeter? Get your mind on something else."

"Right...good thinking." Hale stepped away from the drop pod and jogged over to Cortaro two pods away.

The Mule made a wobbly approach toward the center of the circle, the bulk of Ar'ri and Caas mag-locked to the ship's roof upsetting the pilot's careful landing. The armor siblings slid off the top and landed hard on the spike, their double-barreled gauss cannons charged and ready.

"No enemy contact," Caas said. "I don't know if that's supposed to be a good sign or a bad sign."

The Mule set down and lowered its ramp. Torni and Ibarra pushed the bulky jump engine out and stopped a few yards from the ship. Stalks rose from Torni's back, serving as additional hands as she ran a power coupling the size of her forearm off the bomb's rig. She jabbed the coupling against the spike, then tapped it several more times.

"Anything I can do to help?" Ibarra asked.

One of Torni's stalks poked him in the chest and pushed him away, then a pair of stalks rose from her leg and back. Their tips glowed red and touched the ground in the same place. A scarlet glow spread through the ground, dissipating to nothing a few yards away.

Hale stopped next to Ibarra and looked him up and down.

"Where's your weapon?" Hale asked.

"Son, if I came down here with one of your boom sticks, it would be more dangerous for you than whatever's in this damn place. I'm a weasel, a manipulator, not a fighter."

"You came down here just to get in the way?"

"This getup is a hell of a lot stronger than you, even with your armor. You want to try moving that damn thing?"

Hale reached for the bomb.

"Don't touch!" Torni snapped. "Sir."

Carius came over, his helm scanning the sky. "Valdar wants an update. They've got activity on their scopes. No more information than that."

"The bomb is ready," Torni said, "but it needs a power source. There's a current of omnium just beneath the surface. I can feel it." Her stalks sank several inches into the spike. Torni's teeth chattered and her head jerked to the side with an uncontrollable tick.

"I-I-I need to get deeper. Time. Something's coming." Her shell lost color and reverted to the swirling fractals of her natural drone exterior. "Something's coming!"

She fell to a knee and pressed her head into her hands. Her fingers melded to her skull...but her stalks kept cutting.

"Incoming," said Hale as he whirled around, his rifle ready...but there was nothing new in the endless haze.

"Up there!" Steuben shouted, pointing into the sky.

A patch of smoky darkness grew in the air. Hale raised his weapon, but a gesture from Carius stopped him from shooting.

"There's nothing there," Carius said. "No heat, nothing else on my optic suite."

"Then why can see I see it?" Ibarra asked.

The smoke descended, flowing into a humanoid shape in a dark cloak, a cowl hiding the face. Its semiopaque form dipped just beneath the surface of the spike between the bomb and the ring of drop pods. Marines and armor leveled their weapons, but none fired.

The cloak resolved into an inky darkness slightly taller than Elias. A star field appeared within it, like Hale was looking into a portal to deep space.

Ibarra stepped in front of Hale's line of fire and walked toward the void figure. Clasping his hands behind his back, he stopped a few yards away.

"Marc Ibarra, official representative of Earth, the Atlantic Union, Karigole People, Dotok Ranked Assembly, Ruhaald Queendoms and..." Ibarra's head canted to the side, then he snapped his fingers. "The Qa'Resh! Don't think I forgot anyone else."

An arm flowed up and a distended skeletal hand made of total darkness pointed at Torni.

+Stop.+

The word hit Hale's mind like a thunderclap, harder than the General's words back on Phoenix.

"Now, now, let's tone down the volume," Ibarra said. "Not everyone's suited for whatever telepathic headache you're trying to use. If you want to parlay, then you do it without trying to bust their skulls."

The figure shrank, whirls of smoke twisting tighter and tighter. A perfect mirror copy of Ibarra stepped out of the smoke, its surface gleaming black like it had been carved from obsidian.

"You will stop," the Xaros Ibarra said,

mimicking his accent but adding a deep resonance to the words. "The device will consume your galaxy just as our home was destroyed. You will stop."

"That's...interesting. Maybe you didn't hear me earlier. I'm kind of a big deal back where I come from. I'm going to need to talk to someone a little higher on the Xaros totem pole. You strike me as a...what did you call it, Torni? A Minder. How about you get Keeper down here. I'd love to finally get to talk to him."

The face of Ibarra's dark mirror contorted in rage. "They will not speak with you! The Xaros are pure. I will suffer your corruption."

"Well, this corruption's got a gun to their head and if your boss wants to work something out...he'd better do it in person." Ibarra crossed his arms and the two stared each other down. Ibarra's foot tapped against the spike.

"Have it your way." Ibarra raised a hand. "Set the timer, my girl. This is starting to bore—"

The Xaros snarled. Its form grew taller as tendrils of dark steam rose from its limbs and it morphed into an armored form like the General...but its plates were of the darkest night. A crown of stars circled its head. The High King's three eyes bore down on Ibarra.

"That's more like it," Ibarra said. "I spent a long time wondering what you were really like, where you came from." He raised his arms to the Apex. "It's not bad."

The High King bent down, his arms touching the floor, elbows out like a bat, face level with Ibarra.

"Leave. Take your weapon and leave. My servants are within reach of your world. Leave and I will spare your planet." The High King's voice rumbled like boulders down an avalanche.

"You want a lot of trust," Ibarra said.

"Accept my offer and take my protection. My servants will flood the galaxy and eradicate every last vestige of life if I do not stop them. Destroy the Apex and the drones will finish what they started. Destroy the Apex and the nothing will wash over every star in the galaxy. All that you are, all that you could ever be, will be rendered down to ash and swept away if you *do not leave.*"

"You could have come in peace." Hale

lowered his rifle and approached the High King. "Instead, you sent your drones to destroy everything they found. How many races, how many countless billions, cried out for mercy? Now you want to compromise?"

"The General acted separately from us. His mistakes are not ours," the High King said. "There can be an accord."

"Liar!" Torni shouted. "One of your kind, Minder, showed me the truth. The Xaros are nothing but conquest, control. I've felt your gestalt, seen inside your soul. You will never let us live." She picked the power coupling up off the ground and fed the tip into the hole she'd burned through the spike.

The High King rose back to his full height. "The Xaros will soon possess the secret to immortality. We will share it...but you must leave. Now."

"Buddy," Ibarra said, shaking his head, "I've traded too much of my soul for this." He tapped the side of his metal head. "I wouldn't wish it on anyone else."

"You have no idea what we're offering...an

escape from the inevitable darkness. Eternal life as gods! Accept my offer and you will ascend far higher than your race could ever imagine."

"You murdered my parents," Hale said. "You murdered everyone we knew and loved on Earth. If we join you, then we betray them. All of them."

"How's your poetry?," Ibarra asked, backing up slightly, "'Look upon my works, ye mighty," Ibarra pointed his hand toward Torni, "and despair.' Activate the bomb, if you please, my dear."

"You will die," the High King said. "No matter what you do here, the Earth will burn. The galaxy will be an empty tomb until the last star burns away. You are nothing!"

"But in their last moments," said Ibarra as a smile spread across his face, "the Xaros looked down on a few mere men and women...and begged to live. If you ever expected mercy, you should have shown some."

Torni slapped a button on the bomb and the jump engine came to life with a hiss. Light crept up the power coupling and into the jump engine. A dull whine filled the air.

The High King vanished in a wisp of smoke.

"Mr. Ibarra," Hale said, "I'm honestly surprised you didn't try to cut a deal."

"There are worse things in the world than defeat, compromise with evil being one of them. Besides, you or Elias would have shot me in the back if I tried to weasel out of setting off the bomb."

"No." Elias raised his shoulder-mounted Gatling cannon and got the barrels spinning. "I would have torn you limb from limb and hurled the pieces into that star. We've got movement in the distance."

"Shore party, this is Valdar. You've got wormhole activity near your location. How long until the device is ready? I don't know how much longer our ticket through the Key Hole is going to last."

"It's taking in power," Torni said. She had a hand on the bomb, and it shimmered in tune with the device. "But slow. Maybe…fifteen minutes until the tear opens and this place gets erased."

An alert flashed on Hale's visor. A short video loop taken from the *Breitenfeld* showed a dark mass moving along the spike toward their position.

"Torni," Hale said, "what'll happen if the ship

turns her big guns on the spike? Looks like we're going to need some fire support."

"Don't do it," Torni said. "The omnium current runs the whole way through. If the ship blows it to hell, the bomb won't amount to a wet firecracker."

"Movement." Elias extended his left arm and unfolded the aegis shield mounted on his forearm. He braced himself between a pair of drop pods and let off controlled bursts from his twin gauss cannons.

A screech rose from the fog.

Hale took cover against a drop pod and saw a dark mass of writhing limbs appear out of the haze.

"Open fire!" Hale zoomed in on the forward edge of the closing enemy, midnight-colored elongated creatures that looked like Xaros drones but were covered in dense fur and fleshy stalks tipped with fanged mouths. Hale shot one with a low-powered blast. The round burst it apart like a dropped egg and continued through two more of the creatures. Dark fluid oozed out of the dismembered sections, boiling away to nothing within seconds.

Hundreds more poured out of the fog in a

seemingly endless tide of gibbering mouths and pounding limbs.

Ar'ri and Caas brought their shoulder-mounted Gatling guns up and unleashed a torrent of bullets that annihilated the forward edge of the horde. Orozco stepped between them and locked his rear leg to ground. The barrels on his own heavy gauss cannon spun up and he added to the weight of fire.

Hale couldn't hear Orozco shouting for joy, but he saw the Spaniard's mouth open and his wide eyes.

The rest of the armor destroyed entire swathes of the enemy, but the tide didn't relent. The report of gauss weapons from every Marine and armor came through like the pounding of a hundred drummers. The forward edge crept closer, clambering over the blasted chunks of their dead.

"*Breitenfeld*?" Hale said through the tenuous IR connection to the ship. "We need fire support. I can't see where the enemy's coming from. Hit danger close, toward the base of the spike from our position. How copy?"

Elias' Gatling cannon ceased firing, but the

barrels kept spinning. Out of ammo. Elias released the mag lock on his Excalibur blade and drew it off his shoulder. He slammed the pommel against his shield twice.

The enemy surged forward as the weight of fire from the armor faded away.

"*Breitenfeld?* Damn it. Torni, whoever's in the Mule, get comms with the ship and—" A wolf-sized creature landed next to Hale and struck at him with a pair of snapping mouths. He slapped a stalk aside then jammed his barrel against its body and blew a hole the size of his fist through the thing. He kicked it away and saw Elias stomp another one into paste. One of the Xaros wolves skittered up Elias' back and tore at the base of his neck with clawed forelimbs.

Hale blasted the wolf off Elias, who didn't seem to notice as his sword cleaved through three more with a single stroke.

A thunderclap broke through the sky. Two blazing streaks shot down and struck the spike beyond the fog. A tidal wave of overpressure swept toward Hale and knocked him off his feet. The *Breitenfeld*'s rail cannons were designed to wreck starships across the airless void. The destructive potential of just one shell used against a terrestrial target rivaled the power of nuclear weapons.

Hale slid across the spike and came to a sudden and ungentle stop against an armor soldier's leg. The snap of gauss weapons relented as the wolves retreated into the fog.

"Captain," Torni said, using a single hand to hoist Hale back onto his feet, "the bomb is a precision piece of equipment held together with duct tape and profanity. The blasts from the *Breit*'s guns are not helping."

"But it still works, right?"

"The power drain just slowed to—"

"Elias!" Bodel pointed his sword toward the fog.

A spear-shaped throng of wolves burst out of the haze and bulldozed over Elias...and continued straight toward the bomb. Hale fired from the hip, striking several of the wolves but failing to stem the tide.

A flash of red light stung Hale's eyes, leaving a painful afterglow. He staggered against Bodel as shouts from his Marines filled his ears. His vision cleared moments later.

A Xaros drone—Torni—floated a few feet in the air, stalks bent toward the prostrate Elias. A burnt carpet of wolves dissipated into the air. The smell of cut grass mixed with ammonia assaulted Hale's senses.

Ar'ri ran to Elias, his footsteps thundering against the floor. The Dotok reached into the scorched mass and lifted Elias up with the snap of caramelized flesh. Elias wiped blackened bits from his optics then recovered his Excalibur blade. He raised the guard to his face in a salute toward Torni.

A tremor rumbled through the spike as the fog lifted. Glittering canyons marked where the *Breitenfeld*'s rail cannons hit home. A warning icon appeared on Hale's visor.

"We're losing air pressure," he said. "Everyone button up."

Hale locked his suit away from the thinning atmosphere and felt relief as the smell of antiseptic air replaced the odor of burnt Xaros wolves.

Torni descended to the ground and reformed

into her human shape, marred by cracks up and down her body.

"You OK?" he asked.

"Sort of. Nothing works right anymore." Torni glanced over at the bomb, then ran to it. She pressed one hand into a mass of fiber-optic cables at one end as her fingers elongated and sank into the machine's innards. Her head shook from side to side over and over again.

"Torni? Something wrong?"

"Captain!" Bailey called to him through the IR. *"Got something on the scope."*

A vid feed of the distant craters came onto his visor. Tall Xaros in the same armor as the General, but in a wide range of colors, crawled from the blasted holes onto the floor of the spike.

"*Breitenfeld* fire control," Hale said, "repeat last mission."

"No," Torni said, the word rippling off her shell, "I can barely hold the bomb together now. Another quake and...I don't know what will happen. We might lose the tear."

"Belay that order," Hale sent to the ship. He

looked up and didn't see a flash from the ventral cannons. "Bailey, what're they doing?"

"Bunch of the big wankers just standing around with their thumbs up their…here they come. 'Bout thirty. Want me to introduce them to Bloke?"

"No, your rifle might foul up the bomb." Thirty Xaros just like the General. He'd barely managed to beat one on Earth with four armor and a well-laid trap. The odds did not look good.

"Torni, how long?"

"I can't…seconds. Hours. Leave, sir. I will do this."

"Leave you behind? Again?" Hale shook his head.

A scarlet beam struck the ground in front of the bomb and ripped a foot-deep furrow through the spike floor. Tiny needles of crystal flared up and bounced off Hale's armor.

"Phalanx! Form up around the bomb," said Colonel Carius as he stepped in front of Hale and unfurled his aegis shield. A second blast came out of the fog and clipped the side of the shield, missing Torni by inches. Carius' Templars stood shoulder to shoulder with the colonel, adding their shields to the wall.

"Fall back! Everyone behind the shields," Hale shouted. The Hussars joined Carius' left flank, the Iron Hearts to his right, keeping a small gap between them as Marines filled in and took cover behind the thick aegis plates.

A muted thunderclap broke through the thinning atmosphere when Bailey fired her rail rifle from the top of a drop pod.

"Bailey!" Cortaro peered around Ar'ri's shield.

"Three of them were aiming right for me," she said. "Didn't hit the spike so no worries—"

A red beam smashed through the drop pod and sent Bailey flying into the air. She landed hard, her rifle still grasped in one hand. She lurched to her feet and made for the phalanx.

More Xaros attacks battered the shield wall, dissipating against the aegis shields with a hiss after each strike.

Cortaro pushed Ar'ri's shield wide and waved her over. She jinked to the side as she ran, ducking beneath a beam aiming for the shield gap.

"Come on!" Cortaro yelled to her.

A blood red beam clipped her shoulder and Bailey screamed then pitched forward.

Cortaro ran from the protective wall. Leaping over a Xaros disintegration beam, he grabbed Bailey by a carry strap on her back.

"Covering fire!" Hale wedged his muzzle between shields and shot a high-powered gauss round at the distant foe. Taking more careful aim, he hit one of the Xaros dead center. The round bounced off the armor with a shower of sparks and no other effect.

Cortaro dragged Bailey into the phalanx. The armor on her left shoulder fused into a solid lump. Yarrow flipped her onto her un-wounded side and pressed an auto-injector against a port on her neck armor. Tufts of air spat from the damaged armor.

"Pulse is weak. Suit's losing integrity," Yarrow said. "I need to get her to the Mule's atmo chamber before she goes hypoxic."

Hale looked over at the Mule, which had attracted no attention from the Xaros.

"They're advancing," Carius said. The colonel drew his Excalibur blade and held it close to his chest.

"Not yet, Yarrow." Hale grabbed Standish by the shoulder. The three specially made bullets on his chest glittered within their harness.

"Lock and load." Hale pointed to the Xaros-killer munitions.

Standish slipped a round into his grenade launcher and ran an auxiliary power line from a pack on his belt to his rifle. A mosquito whine broke through the crash of beams against aegis shields.

"Torni promised this wouldn't blow my hands off." Standish checked the power level then banged a fist against Elias' side.

"Move over, big boy. Guess who gets to save the day." Standish leaned over and took aim through a slight gap, then a sunburst of golden light roared out of Standish's muzzle. The Marine sidestepped away and reloaded.

The round hit true, blasting through a Xaros master's midsection and severing its legs. The upper torso flailed against the spike for a second as its essence steamed away. The other masters stopped and watched as their peer died.

Standish's next shot blew a master's head

clean off. He let off a high-pitched chuckle as he slammed his third and final round into the breach.

The Xaros backed off, firing wildly as they retreated.

"Let me tell you something," Ibarra said to Hale. "I spent a lot of years dealing with rich and powerful bullies. It's always something to see what happens the first time they get a punch to the face. The Xaros never fought someone that could hurt them before. War doesn't seem as much when fun when you're playing for keeps, does it, you bastards?"

"Sir! I've got to move her," Yarrow said. He had Bailey on a litter. Her skin had a blue sheen to it and her eyes fluttered.

"First Sergeant, get her to the Mule. Standish, hold your last shot." Hale peeked around a shield.

A dark curtain rose out of the craters. A talon of solid smoke snatched one of the retreating Xaros and lifted it into the air. The talon crushed the master as glowing slime spilled from the claws. The rest of the Xaros stopped in their tracks.

More masters emerged from the craters, each carrying scythes as tall as they were.

The three-eyed face of the High King appeared in the dark wall, and a claw tip stabbed toward the phalanx.

"Shoot the big one?" Standish asked.

"Don't miss," Hale said.

Standish unleashed his final Excalibur round. It hit the High King in his left eye, slapping his face to the side. A roar that sent shivers through Hale's body echoed from the distance, then the High King vanished into nothing.

The Xaros ran for the phalanx.

"Think I got it?" Standish's rifle began to gyrate in his hands. "Bad. Bad!" He chucked the weapon through the gap...only to see it go about two feet before it caught on the end of the power line and bounced back at him.

Elias covered the weapon with his shield and absorbed the blast. Sparking hunks of what remained of Standish's rifle scattered across the ground. Elias got his shield up just as a trio of disintegration beams reached the chink in the phalanx's armor.

"Thanks, big guy," Standish said. "We're even for that save in the hospital."

"No." Elias shook his helm. "We will never be even."

"You think they know we're out of silver bullets?" Ibarra asked.

"No, I think they don't care. The High King made it obvious what'll happen if they don't stop the bomb. Looks like fighting us is more appealing than certain death," Hale said.

Torni gasped as she withdrew her hand from the bomb and shook it back into shape.

"It started." She backed away, fear writ across her cracked face. "The tear, the annihilation wave, it will be here soon. Oh, God, what have we done?"

The Mule rose off the ground and flew toward them.

"Torni, can the Xaros still stop the bomb from going off?" Hale asked.

"Yes. If they rip it apart before it ignites, this will all be for nothing. We've got twenty minutes, maybe less."

Hale looked up at the *Breitenfeld*, then to all the armor and his Marines around him. There was no way the ship could send another transport down for all of them and still have time to escape.

"Get her back to the ship," Carius said. "Prep the *Breitenfeld* to go up if we can't hold down here."

"Wait…there has to be a way." Hale held up a hand as his mind raced. "We can…we all go home or nobody goes home!"

"Ken." Elias grabbed him by the arm. "Torni is the mission now. We'll buy you the time. You take the chance. Now get out of here."

"That's an order, *Captain*," Colonel Carius said.

The Mule swung around. Cortaro stood on the ramp, beckoning to the Marines.

"Go! Get out of here!" Hale grabbed Standish and pushed him toward the Mule. Standish caught himself midway and held his ground.

"Sir, all or nothing," Standish said.

Elias leaned toward Hale. A panel flipped open on the armor's chest and Elias' face emerged from a milky white gloom. Honey-colored eyes misty with cataracts stared at Hale.

"Go," Elias said. "Live well. You do not need to die here. We will pay the price. We are armor."

Hale knew what he had to do next, even if it broke his heart.

"Captain," Steuben growled, "I will carry you if necessary."

"Get on the boat," Hale said to the Karigole. "It was an honor, Elias."

The panel snapped shut and Elias slapped the flat of his blade against his knee, knocking flecks of Xaros-wolf away.

Hale ran for the Mule. Torni, Ibarra and the rest of his Marines were already aboard. He jumped onto the ramp as the ship lifted into the sky.

CHAPTER 18

Elias watched as the Xaros masters advanced toward the phalanx. Two flanks emerged from the main thrust of the approaching mass, now several hundred strong, and moved to encircle the bomb. The enemy had stopped firing once it was obvious the aegis shields made a mockery of the disintegration beams.

"Tight circle around the bomb," Carius said. "We are the anvil upon which the enemy will break."

The Iron Hearts took up the right side of the circle, blades ready. The Hussars to one side held their *kopia* spears low against their shields.

"Kallen would have wanted to be here," Bodel said.

"She is here," Elias said, "watching. Judging. We had best earn our place beside her."

Caas scraped the edge of her sword along the edge of her shield. Her back foot thumped against the ground.

"After our parents died," she said, "Ar'ri was all I have left. The Dotok aren't in the habit of adopting orphans. That's what everyone from Takeni had become, a people without a home, no one to care for us. But you, Earth, took us all in. You let us become armor. I still don't understand why."

"Any that shed their blood with us become our brothers. There is no more precious gift." Elias tightened his grip on his sword as Xaros masters came out of the gloom.

"Thank you, Elias, Bodel," Ar'ri said. "Our parents died to save us. We pass on their gift to all our people and to yours."

The Xaros quickened their pace. They raised their weapons—scythes bearing white-hot blades— charging in silence.

"Be glorious, my armor," Carius said. "Or we will not be remembered."

Elias slammed the hilt of his sword against his shield twice, opened his suit's speakers, lifted his sword high, and gave a war cry that shook the shards of crystal around his feet. Bodel matched his fury, then the rest of the armor joined in.

A Xaros leapt up, its scythe poised high to strike against Elias as it fell. Elias swept his Excalibur blade up and cut the attacker from armpit to neck. The distinct parts fell to Elias' side. The armor snapped the blade out in a reverse swing and broke through the next Xaros' scythe and slashed it across the throat. The master's head flipped back, light spilling out of the near decapitation. Elias kicked it aside.

The Xaros embedded a pair of scythe tips into Bodel's shield arm and pulled him off-balance. Elias slashed his blade down and severed the wrists of the two Xaros working against his brother, then fired his gauss cannons into the Xaros, knocking them both back and into the press of masters joining the fight.

He caught a glint out of the corner of his eye and ducked behind his shield as the shaft of a scythe whacked against it. The blade tip cut across Elias' back. His back flared in pain, matching the damage to his armor. Elias rammed his blade into the Xaros' chest and lifted it off the ground as the guard caught against the enemy's armored skin.

The Xaros grabbed at the blade, glowing viscera pouring from the wound. Elias hurtled it headfirst into the ground then slammed a foot against its dented head and slid his weapon free. Crushing his heel down on the Xaros' skull, he felt a satisfying crack through his armor.

An unarmed Xaros leapt at him and got both arms wrapped around Elias' shield. It twisted around, dodging a chop from Elias, and wrested the shield arm aside, exposing Elias to a Xaros carrying an energy weapon.

A blast of energy as thick as Elias' neck burst from the weapon.

Bodel lunged to the side and got his shield between his fellow Iron Heart and the red bolt. The impact slapped the shield against Elias' helm and spun Bodel around. The shield broke into pieces and scattered across the ground in burning fragments.

The Xaros with the disintegration beam

swung the weapon toward the gap in the phalanx. Right at the exposed bomb.

Bodel jumped up and took the Xaros' next shot in the chest. The aegis plating on Bodel's armor dampened most of the hit. Most. The disintegration beam broke through his breastplate and struck the man within. His armor stopped. The shoulders slumped forward and his Excalibur blade clattered to the ground.

Elias roared and hurled his sword at the Xaros that just killed his brother. The weapon pierced through the scythe and ripped through the alien, carrying it off its feet and into another Xaros.

Elias grabbed Bodel's sword, refusing to look into the burning crater at the armor's heart. The phalanx tightened as Adamczyk fell to a scythe that pierced through his womb, killing him instantly.

Rage coursed through Elias as he struck out at a Xaros in sky-blue armor. His weapon smashed through the Xaros' block and embedded in its shoulder. Elias slid the blade free, leaving a deeper cut. The Xaros' arm held on by a thread as it tried to retreat.

"It is time for you to know pain!" Elias jabbed the edge of his shield into another Xaros' face and slashed it across the belly. "It is time for you to know fear!"

He parried a swing and rammed the tip of his blade into the attacker's neck, popping its head into the air with a flick of his wrist.

A scythe bit into his sword arm and ripped down the armor. His body screamed in pain, but Elias kept his grip. A blow smashed into the side of his helm, shattering half his optics. A Xaros stomped on the flat of his blade, jerking it out of his hand and pinning it to the ground.

Elias looked up at a Xaros in ivory armor as it readied a killing blow, eyes blazing with hatred.

A *kopia* slammed through the Xaros' chest and sent it staggering backward. Elias grabbed the Hussar's spear by the shaft, ripped it free, and tossed it back to Ferenz, who directed the momentum into another enemy.

"Ar'ri!" Caas shouted.

Her brother, his armor pierced by four scythes, fell forward and into a scrum of Xaros who hacked at the Dotok as he lay on the ground.

Elias grabbed Caas and pulled her back before she could rush to help him.

"Hold the line!" Elias took a hit to his shield that pierced through the back of the aegis plate. He twisted aside and ripped the weapon out of the enemy's hands then cut it from shoulder to shoulder with a reverse slash.

A sudden chill gripped Elias by the heart. His armor's systems flickered and gave him impossible readings. He felt a pull against his armor taking him back...toward the bomb.

"It's starting," Caas said.

Armor plates rose from the trail of dead Xaros, coalescing into a hulking monster with a scaled cloak and a starry crown. The High King, one eye cracked and dark from Standish's bullet, extended a palm toward the bomb. Elias and Caas joined their shields together and took the brunt of the blast that ripped through a score of Xaros masters before it hit them.

Elias braced his feet against the ground as his shield went white-hot. When the pressure relented, he swept his shield aside. Caas fell to the ground, the right half of her armor a blackened mass of fused metal, her blade seared and broken.

"Caas?"

A screech of defiance came from the High King.

Elias looked back and saw the bomb was still intact. The air wavered around the device as the fabric of reality began to unravel. Carius and three others fought back-to-back mere feet from it.

The High King's other hand began to glow.

Elias sprinted forward. He dropped his damaged shield aside and gripped his blade with both hands. Sidestepping a grasping hand, he roared...loud enough to take the High King's attention away from the bomb.

The Iron Heart leapt into the air and straight at the High King, burying his weapon in the High King's neck. The blade caught against the star-filled cloak. Elias held on as the High King reared back with a screech.

"Look at me, monster!" Elias grabbed a handful of cloak and held on tight. He raised his anchor foot and stabbed the diamond-tipped spike through the High King's chest.

"I'm not afraid of you!" Elias wrenched his blade until it shattered. He drew the broken blade back and stabbed it into one of the High King's eyes. The Xaros lord opened his mouth to scream, but there was no sound. Color drained away from the world.

Elias looked to the bomb. A glut of absolute darkness fountained out of the bomb and fell over Carius and the rest of the fighters. The annihilation wave flowed free, erasing everything it touched.

Elias twisted the High King's head toward their shared doom.

"I know where I'm going," Elias growled. "I know who waits for me. Can you say the same?"

****

Valdar stood still as a statue against the side of his holo tank, watching as the annihilation wave consumed the spike like a hungry cancer, leaving nothing but the abyss in its wake. Within the tank a single track moved at a snail's pace toward the *Breitenfeld*—the Mule from the surface carrying Hale and his Marines.

The annihilation wave spread up and down the spike rapidly. It crept upwards slowly, but Valdar saw it accelerating.

"How long until the wave catches up with us?" Valdar asked.

"We don't have any kind of readings in it," Geller said. "Anything that touches it…doesn't come back. No radar, laser range sounding, nothing."

"Helm, set course for the wormhole portal. Engine room, can you still get us out of here?"

"Waiting for your word," Levin answered.

The annihilation wave stretched upward, undulating.

"Wait for it," Valdar said.

The Mule drew closer, its speed far too high for a safe landing.

"Deck, prep for emergency landing. Get the nets and catch lines ready."

Valdar didn't pay attention to the response as his ship drew within range to activate the jump engine and escape the nothingness coming to claim the *Breitenfeld*.

"Come on, Hale," Valdar whispered. He brought up a video feed of the aft flight-deck doors. He saw the annihilation wave, pale light reflecting off the writhing mass of night, through the feed beneath his ship.

"Come on, son."

"Captain!" Ericson screamed at him. "It's accelerating!"

The Mule zoomed into the flight deck...and careened off the ceiling. Valdar felt the impact through the floor.

"Now! Engine room! Now!" Valdar shouted into the IR.

As everything went white, Valdar wasn't sure if the jump engines had ignited or if he was about to meet his maker.

CHAPTER 19

Stacey held her arms at her sides, her knees bent as she floated near the inner edge of the Key Hole. She'd spent several seconds in an undignified panic when she realized she was in the void without a proper vac suit. Her body was a nigh-indestructible technological marvel, but the mind within still remembered the horror of exposure to total vacuum.

Malal floated next to her, his knees folded into a lotus position, the very picture of calm.

In the distance, between Sletari and the Key Hole, the battle between the combined human and Ruhaald fleets continued against the Xaros swarm.

+Hurry, Malal. People are dying,+ she said.

A golden lattice worked across his featureless

face. His fingers twitched ever so slightly.

Stacey looked to the center of the Key Hole, unsure what effect the *Breitenfeld*'s return—if she returned—would have on her and her charge.

The lattice fizzled away.

+The Engineer's essence was more complicated than I anticipated, but I have a solution. It lacks grace and is inefficient, but it meets your needs.+

+You can destroy the drones? How?+

Malal held a palm to Stacey. +Crystal.+

Stacey took a small, eight-sided, clear crystal, used by the Qa'Resh to store and transmit enormous amounts of data, and handed it over. Malal let it bounce within a loose cage made by his fingers. It touched his thumb and froze. Green light filled the crystal, twinkling like a star seen through a night sky. Malal nudged the crystal back to her.

+Send the commands to your toy in the Key Hole. The Xaros structure will do the rest.+

Stacey held the crystal between her fingertips. A slight tremor passed through her hand and into the rest of her body.

+Ben?+

+*Standing by.*+

+I have something for...what's happening?+
Light exploded across her eyes as an electric jolt
coursed through her body.

When she recovered, she found Malal
gripping her wrist with one hand and holding the
now-clear crystal in the other.

+You could have warned me.+ She pulled her
hand back gently, not wanting to go tumbling through
the void from the slightest bit of transferred
momentum.

The basalt spikes making up the many rings of
the Key Hole stopped moving...then pointed their
tips toward the raging battle. The tips shivered for a
moment, then folded back to their prior
configuration.

+What did you do?+ Stacey asked.

+Watch.+

The explosions of void fighters and the flash
of disintegration beams and quadrium munitions died
away. A shadow passed over Sletari and stopped over
the star. The shadow grew fainter and fainter.

+I could not access the self-destruct code Torni once held, but I found a fragment of source code used for their aggression response matrix.+

+Don't be cute with me. What did you do?+

+The drones' primary function was to annihilate all signs of active intelligent life. I changed it to attack strong sources of radiation. The Xaros were photonic-based lifeforms. The code for 'life' and the energy wavelength of ultraviolet radiation were very similar. The drones are resistant to malicious code from any source but the Crucibles.+

+You tricked the drones into attacking the sun?+

+Correct. This is not the complete solution, but it is proof I have what you want.+ Malal grasped the empty crystal until it glowed green. He pressed it to his chest and drew it into himself. +To destroy every last drone in the galaxy, you must connect to the Crucible network and upload what I put in the crystal. It will travel through every last gate and propagate at the speed of light in all directions. Every drone it touches will fly into the nearest star.+

+What are you waiting for? Give me the

crystal now. There are drones heading for Earth. I can get back through the other Crucible and—+

+No. I can fulfill my end of the bargain. You will take me to my ascension and prove you can fulfill your promise. I see the anger building in your matrix. You must learn to control your atavistic urges. They don't suit one so advanced as you. Destroy me with the governor and you will destroy the crystal too. Then your chances of surviving the Xaros, even if the *Breitenfeld* succeeds, are almost impossible. The drones threatening Earth are weeks away. Take me to my reward now and you will have the crystal and your planet will be saved.+

Stacey's hands clenched in anger.

+I hate you. I know what you've done. Seen firsthand the murders that propelled you and your kind to immortality. Despite everything you've done…you have been true to our agreement. You, the vile, selfish…demon. Yet who betrayed humanity? Stabbed us in the back when we needed them the most? Our own flesh-and-blood kind, the ones facing the same threat of extinction in the Xaros. The Toth turned on Bastion then tried to trick us during negotiations. The Vishrakath destroyed the Alliance because their influence was waning. The Ruhaald and Naroosha betrayed us on Earth, and for what? The chance to live a little longer against the Xaros using human slave soldiers?+

+You hate me for what I am and for what my loyalty says about your kind. If it means anything to you, I don't care.+

Malal grabbed her by the hand and propelled them both over the inner edge of the Key Hole.

The *Breitenfeld* emerged seconds later. The tips of her ventral cannons were mere stubs, and the long magnetic acceleration vanes ended in gleaming points like they'd been cut by an impossibly large scalpel.

+They succeeded...and survived. Much to my surprise.+ Malal dragged her toward the open flight deck. +Come. I've waited a long time for this. Only one thing remains between me and apotheosis...and revenge.+

****

Hale held his head back, braced against the

Mule's restraints. He heard the *tink tink tink* of heat-warped metal and opened his eyes. The Mule's ramp was gone, ripped away in the rough landing and lying on the *Breitenfeld*'s flight deck. The top gauss turret pressed through the split metal remnants of the ceiling. His Marines sat in acceleration chairs along the walls, all looking groggy from their sudden stop within the ship.

"Give me an up." Hale slapped the emergency release and took a wobbly step on the deck.

"Sick bay's got a crash cart on the way." Yarrow tapped the side of his helmet then rushed to the atmo chamber against the fore of the cargo bay. A coffin-sized hatch slid up and Yarrow slid Bailey and her litter out. Orozco grabbed one end and carried her out of the Mule. They met a team of corpsmen on the flight deck who rushed Bailey away as Yarrow followed.

"Think she'll be OK?" Standish asked.

"Her vitals stabilized," said Cortaro as he removed his helmet and took a deep breath. "Besides, she's Australian. Nothing kills them."

Hale took his helmet off and went to the

broken edge of the Mule. The Key Hole spun in the distance. He waited, unsure if that nightmare wave was going to follow them through the gate. A thought came to him as he waited, a truth he didn't think he'd ever really confront.

He felt Steuben's heavy steps approach.

"It's over, isn't it?" Hale asked.

Steuben put his hand on Hale's shoulder. "Well done, Captain Hale. Well done."

"Elias…"

"They fought the final battle and won. Few warriors earn that. Do not spoil their victory with grief," the Karigole said.

Hale shrugged the hand away.

The inner ring of the Key Hole cracked into halves. The crack jumped to the next ring and the next. Broken lines splintered off the cracks and individual thorns fell away like needles from a dead pine. Hale, his Marines and the sailors on the flight deck watched in stunned awe as the Key Hole burned away like a destroyed drone.

"The war's over?" Standish stepped onto the deck and gazed at the void where the Key Hole had been. "Hey! The war's over!" He raised his arms in triumph and let out a cheer.

"Permission to strangle him," Cortaro said.

A cheer spread across the flight deck. Sailors hugged and cried tears of joy. Orozco wrapped an arm around a female deckhand's waist and said words lost to the celebration. She grabbed him by the neck and kissed him.

"No. Let them have this." Hale sat on a bench and pressed his face to his palms.

"Ken?" Valdar asked through Hale's earpiece. *"What happened down there?"*

"One wounded, on the way to medical. The armor, all of the armor...missing in action."

"Good job, son. That you brought back so many...proud of you. Don't get too comfortable. Seems this isn't over yet."

"What? The Apex is gone. What's left? Who's telling us there's more to do?"

"Little help here?" Ibarra, still in his harness, waved to Cortaro. The first sergeant undid the restraints and grabbed Ibarra by the arms. Cortaro jerked his hands back and cursed in Spanish.

"Sorry, still getting used to the new me." Ibarra fumbled out of the acceleration chair then went to the ragged edge of the Mule's cargo space. He looked over the celebration then sighed.

"Ibarra," said Hale, dropping his hands to his knees and looking up at the man, "I thought you'd be...happy. We won, the Xaros are gone, Earth is safe. You've been working for this longer than anyone alive."

"There was a cost, son. I made almost every living human pay the ultimate price to get us here. Decades of lies, arranging conflicts, killing those who couldn't be bribed or blackmailed to play my game. There may have been another way, a better way, but I did the best I could...and it isn't over yet."

Stacey and Malal flew into the cargo bay. Their presence seemed to suck the joy away from the nearby crewmen. Stacey looked at her grandfather and nodded.

"Call the captain down here," Ibarra said. "I want the both of you to see what happens next."

CHAPTER 20

Hale stood next to Valdar at the edge of the flight deck, watching the last of the Ruhaald ships enter the Crucible. Streaks of fire burnt across Sletari as the first fragments of the world's obliterated moon succumbed to gravity.

Stacey and Ibarra stood a few feet away, one on either side of Malal. Stacey's worried face and Ibarra's stoicism bothered Hale. The two were architects of the war effort...yet both looked like they'd suffered a great defeat. What was bothering them?

"There's no chance we can ever explore Sletari," Hale said. "All that technology, all that history will be lost forever."

Stacey clasped her hands behind her back.

"This isn't the only world Malal's people left behind," she said. "There will be more for us to find. The Crucible already sent Admiral Garret and our fleet back to Earth. Ben will deposit the Ruhaald back to their home world, then we can be on our way."

"This Crucible has a few more hours before a hunk of rock the size of Mount Everest hits it," Valdar said. "Garret said you'd share our next mission once the Ruhaald were away. I'm waiting."

The wormhole closed around the final alien ship and the *Breitenfeld* moved forward with a rumble of engines.

"Garret didn't tell you," Ibarra huffed, "because he didn't know how you'd react. I've brought us all this far. Trust me for a little bit longer."

"This is my ship, Ibarra." Valdar's face clenched in anger. He held his voice low to keep the flight-deck crew from overhearing him. "I'm responsible for my crew and if you think you're going to just—"

"Yes, the *Breitenfeld* is yours," Ibarra said, waving a dismissive hand, "but her jump engines are mine."

A Qa'Resh probe flew into the flight deck and came to rest in Stacey's palm. She closed a fist around it and cocked her head to the side.

"We're ready," she said.

A wormhole opened within the Crucible.

"No, we are not your playthings," Valdar said. He opened an IR channel to engineering. "Levin, shut down the jump engine."

"I...I can't, sir. I'm locked out of the system."

"See if Torni can—" the IR channel cut with the snap of Ibarra's fingers.

"Oh, how I missed that," Ibarra chuckled. "Like I said, the jump engines are mine, Valdar. I actually kind of like you, which is why I'm not giving you any say in what happens next. Plausible deniability. The ability to sleep at night. You'll thank me years from now."

The ship entered the wormhole.

****

Hale rubbed his eyes as the wormhole faded

away. They were orbiting a planet with dense jungles and pale seas. Around the equator, a massive structure ringed the entire planet. Running lights from thousands on top of thousands of ships swarmed around the belt.

A starship several times the size of the *Breitenfeld* undocked from a nearby space station, a ship the kind Hale had seen up close and personal. A Toth dreadnought set an intercept course for the *Breitenfeld*.

"Toth'anon." Stacey raised a hand to the world. "Home to hundreds of billions…hundreds of billions of sentient beings. It is enough?" she asked Malal.

"More than enough. Let me slip. I have held my hunger for far too long."

Stacey closed her eyes a moment, then said, "Go."

The governor fell from Malal's chest and clanged against the deck. A single, clear gem rattled inside the many hoops bound into a sphere.

Malal stepped through the force field and streaked away, straight for the incoming Toth dreadnought.

Hale could have sworn he heard laughing in the distance.

"Ibarra, what are we doing?" Valdar asked.

"Not you, my friend." Ibarra put a hand on Stacey's shoulder. "The two of us, the Qa'Resh, we made this bargain with Malal. The thing about dealing with the devil…he always comes to collect."

"Sir, we're being hailed," Ericson said.
"A…Supreme Overlord Rannik demands to speak to you."

Ibarra and Stacey watched as the burning light that was Malal closed on the dreadnought.

"Put her through." Valdar lifted his arm and a holo screen appeared over his gauntlet. A nervous system suspended within a jar of bubbling fluid writhed before the captain.

"Valdar…I can't say I'm surprised. After you killed Mentiq and removed much of my competition, I decided to leave your meat species alone to grow fat and happy while I consolidated control on Toth'anon. What brings you here? Trade? There really is only one thing I want from you…"

"Sir, Toth ship is powering weapons," Ericson said

through Valdar's earpiece.

"Your presence means the Ruhaald and Naroosha failed," Rannik said. "An inherited business arrangement negotiated between the Vishrakath and Mentiq. Not the deal I would have made but contracts are contracts."

Malal sped toward the tip of the massive Toth ship...and passed right through it. He emerged from the far end seconds later, his light burning brighter as he continued on to the space station.

"The cost overruns in dealing with your species have proved most taxing to my efforts to bring the final few corporations in line. Perhaps we can...what's happening? Why isn't my flagship responding to my commands?"

Malal flew into an open cargo bay and light burst from the station's windows. Malal, his form expanded to the size of a destroyer, made a beeline for Toth'anon.

"No...no...what are we doing?" Hale asked. "We can't do this to them!"

"Valdar? What is that energy reading from your ship?" Rannik said, her tendrils constricted into knots. "What is the *baelor* talking about?"

"Turn it off," Ibarra said. "There's nothing to say to them."

"Valdar! Valdar, we can work out a deal if you'll—" The captain closed the channel.

Valdar drew his pistol and pointed it at Ibarra's temple. Ibarra kept his eyes locked on Malal as it drew closer to the Toth planet.

"Call him back," Valdar said. "The Toth may be our enemies but we do not do this. You understand me, Ibarra? There is no justification for this!"

"The Toth are broken, Isaac," Ibarra said. "Their leaders are addicts, cursed to live off the life essence of others. There's no going back for them."

Stacey looked away, a hand over her mouth.

"Their warriors, their menials, have no concept of rebellion," Ibarra said. "There is no faction to make a separate peace with. The Toth will never stop until they get control of the procedural technology to feed their addiction. We had to choose between a protracted conflict with the Toth—look at their technology, we were lucky they sent such a small fleet the first time they attacked—or to leave it to Malal. This solves two problems. The Toth and Malal."

Steuben ran across the flight deck, short sword in hand. He slid to a stop next to Hale, his yellow eyes burning with hatred.

"Why are we here?" Steuben demanded.

"To end the Toth," Stacey said, "and save the Earth from Xaros drones."

"Ibarra, call him back." Valdar pressed the muzzle toward Ibarra's head but the pistol turned away as it bumped against an invisible force field. Ibarra tapped a puck on his belt.

"Not your decision, Captain." Ibarra clasped his hands behind his back. "Question for you. The Xaros wiped out the Earth, pushed us to the very edge of extinction. In return, we destroyed them—the true Xaros, not their drones. We, humanity, committed xenocide for the sake of our own survival. You had no complaints. Now here we are with one of the last Karigole who suffered as we did, but at the hands of the Toth. Steuben, what should we do?"

Light glinted from Steuben's sword as he

twisted it from side to side.

"You will kill them? All of them?" Steuben asked.

"Yes, we will," Ibarra said dispassionately.

"I remember the fields," the Karigole said, "the endless fields of our dead. You don't know what it's like, to see everything taken away, to know that you are the very last of your people. My centurion, we all took the oath to make the Toth pay. Our lives could not end until the vendetta was paid with Toth blood."

"We killed Mentiq," Hale said. "We saved that village on Nibiru. Isn't that enough? Tell Ibarra that this isn't what you want."

Malal struck the great belt around Toth'anon. A ripple of light spread across the planet like a stone dropped on a still pond.

Steuben shook his head. "Let it happen. Let justice be done, no matter the cost."

"At least someone has sense," Ibarra said.

Valdar lowered his pistol.

"You're both fools," Valdar said. "The only reason you ever had control over Malal was because he was weak. What happens after this? You think he'll stop with the Toth? You destroyed one monster and unleashed another."

"We control Malal because we have what he wants," Stacey said, "the only thing he wants. Letting him do this was the only way we could get him to work against the Xaros." She looked down at the governor and tapped the crystal with a fingertip.

"You think he'll just put that leash back on once he comes back?" Valdar asked. "I'm not taking the chance. Engine room...engine room!" Valdar looked at Hale, who tried using his own IR system, then shook his head.

"You really think we'd come this far then start hoping things would go well?" Ibarra asked. "I'm disappointed, Valdar. I thought we knew each other."

The wave of light came back over Toth'anon's horizon, coalescing in the same spot it began. Malal emerged from the planet, blazing with light that cast new shadows behind those watching the planet. The entity's light dimmed as it grew closer.

"It is done," Steuben said. "The Toth are no more."

"The second race humanity has destroyed in less than a day," Stacey said. "Both acts for the sake of our own survival."

"Not just ours." Ibarra nodded to Steuben. "The rest of the galaxy, all those other races that were part of Bastion, they owe us too. But somehow I doubt they'll remember it that way. One era ends, another begins. At least Earth will have the upper hand, for once."

Malal landed next to Stacey, his body pulsating with a dim glow. Toth scales appeared beneath his surface, joined by the ghost of an overlord's nervous system.

"They were enough." Malal's gaze shifted to Hale, Valdar and Steuben. "But I have never drank from human souls…"

Stacey smacked the governor against Malal's chest. It sank a few inches, then caught as Malal issued a low growl.

"You got what you need," she hissed. "You get nothing else. You take this back or you'll never find your door. The Qa'Resh and I swear it." She pressed the governor…and it melded into Malal's body.

Steuben tossed his heirloom sword into the air and through the force field. It went end over end through the void.

"I never thought this day would come," Steuben said.

"Is it worth it?" Hale asked him.

"I have no room in my heart for the Toth. They earned their fate. My time as a warrior is over. I will return to my people, if you will let me."

Hale glanced at Malal. His body had become slightly wider, hands elongated…almost like Mentiq, the Toth overlord he'd seen on Nibiru.

"Something tells me we're not out of the woods yet, Steuben."

A wormhole opened in front of the *Breitenfeld*.

CHAPTER 21

Hale rubbed his eyes as the aftereffects of the wormhole passed.

"I'm really getting sick of this," Hale said. He blinked hard...and saw a gray expanse beyond the *Breitenfeld.* He'd seen one before, when the ship had gone to Bastion after first encountering Malal on Anthalas.

"Where are we, Ibarra?" Valdar asked.

"No idea! Which is the point of the pocket universe the Qa'Resh set up for this sort of thing." Ibarra nudged Stacey with his elbow.

"Right, sorry." She held up a hand and the Qa'Resh probe lifted out of her palm.

"Where is it?" Malal's right foot grew into a clawed Toth foot and scraped the deck. "Where is my reward?"

Hale felt the ship sway as the gray beyond shifted to the side. In the distance, a black hole swung into view. Bands of crystalline rings circled the singularity, spinning through each other with impossible grace. The edges of each ring were distinct fractal patterns that reminded Hale of a snowflake's outer edge. The Qa'Resh city held steady near the construct, itself dwarfed by what danced around the black hole.

"There..." Malal said. "My design. My idea. My work. They locked me away once they had the keys to immortality. Now the path I designed will take me straight to them...and her."

"The code," Stacey said. "The code to defeat the drones. Give it to me now."

"No. I will give it to you at the threshold. Nowhere else."

Blue light reflected off the ceiling. A Qa'Resh rose up, its light filling the flight deck with a sense of peace. Its long crystalline tendrils reached down and formed into two saucer shapes, a small one for Malal, a larger space for the rest standing on the edge of the flight deck.

"Well this is...different." Ibarra tapped the Qa'Resh's surface, then gingerly stepped into the cupped crystal.

"It's not so bad," Stacey said. "Done it once before. They want you to come," she said to Valdar, Hale and Steuben. None of them moved an inch.

"I think it's important for more than just my grandfather and I to see this. Earth, the rest, they'll all want to know what happens here," she said.

The saucer with Malal pulled out of the hangar deck and joined the rest of the tentacles hanging beneath the alien's body.

"Where will it take us?" Hale asked.

Stacey stepped over the lip and sat down. "To answers. To the truth."

Hale climbed in. Valdar and Steuben joined him after Valdar had a brief conversation with Ericson. The saucer moved once Valdar cleared the lip. They passed through the force field, but Hale felt no different. Air, temperature, even the smell of

314

battery packs and hydraulics all stayed the same.

The Qa'Resh pulled them into the mass of tentacles and the world around them went dark.

An elderly man in a white robe appeared in the middle of the room.

"Hale, it is good to see you again. We knew you'd be a part of this," he said.

"What are you..." Blocked memories flooded through Hale's mind. Traveling through the clouds of a gas giant on a sled with Yarrow and Stacey. The same Qa'Resh removing Malal from the corpsman's body. The kind smile of the old man with the same twinkle in his eye that Hale remembered from his grandfather.

"You saw too much when we first met," the Qa'Resh said. "As did Torni. We took steps to protect Bastion in case either of you were ever captured by the Toth...the Xaros' methods of interrogation were more than we anticipated. Forgive us. There's no need for it to happen again."

"I saw you on Sletari, Qa'Resh," Hale said. "That's Malal's world. What is going on between you and that monster?"

"The Qa'Resh are...guilt. Penance. Karma," the old man said. "Before Malal found a path to true immortality, our creators were dying. Even their technology could not stave off entropy forever. Malal found a solution, immortal life at the expense of all other intelligent life in the galaxy. In their haste, in their fear, they chose Malal's path. One, you would consider her Malal's sister, stood in the ashes of civilizations and realized she was wrong. While she hated what her brother had done, she could not destroy him. She sabotaged his ascension and locked him away below Anthalas."

"The Qa'Resh are Malal's...sister?" Valdar asked.

"No, we are her creation. To atone for her race's crimes, she split her existence between this plane and the next. She maintained a vigil against the rise of another power like Malal, sought to guide the emerging races to coexistence. Used us to carry out her will. Galactic powers do not arise quickly. We had millennia to evaluate a race as they developed intelligence and made their first steps through the void. We had time to handle problems correctly.

316

When the Xaros drones first arrived, they spread faster than we could combat. We tried to form alliances to stem the tide, but we failed. We failed over and over again."

The old man folded his hands into his wide sleeves.

"We retreated to buy time, figure out a new strategy. Let the Xaros overwhelm more than half the galaxy while we gathered races at Bastion through our probes. Tried to foster goodwill and cooperation between such different species. Eventually, we came up with the gambit to capture an incomplete Crucible."

"At the cost of almost ten billion people," Ibarra said.

"But our probe, all our technology couldn't complete the device or break into the Xaros network," the old man said.

"So you sent us to break Malal out of jail," Valdar said. "His sister knew he could solve your problem."

"And Malal wanted a family reunion in return," Hale said.

"The choice was difficult," the Qa'Resh said.

"Why are you telling us this?" Stacey asked. "You think you can justify what you did to Earth? What we've done to others?"

"We failed," the Qa'Resh said. "We failed to unite the galaxy through mutual understanding and selfless service. The victory over the Xaros came through guile, sacrifice, coercion. She would ask…given what you've been through…not to lose hope in each other."

"You think because the Xaros are gone the races that are left will tear each other apart, don't you?" Ibarra shook his head. "Of course we'll go to war with each other. The Toth. The Vishrakath. They were in this for themselves and now everything is chaos. The center cannot hold. Anarchy is loosed upon the galaxy."

"But you have conviction," the Qa'Resh said to Valdar. "Humanity showed the galaxy that there can be cooperation. Coexistence."

"And look what that got us," Ibarra said. "It set the Vishrakath against us and put alien ships in our skies. Our cities would have been nuked if a thief and a pair of miscreant knuckle-draggers hadn't got themselves captured by the Ruhaald."

"The only reason this worked," Stacey said, "is because the Qa'Resh, sent by Malal's sister, had compassion. She could have gone off with the rest of her kind, and there would have been nothing to stop the Xaros."

"We ask you to remember this." The Qa'Resh raised an arm and the surrounding darkness parted like a curtain.

They were in a vast amphitheater. Bronze tiles with gently shifting fractals stretched to a dome wall that changed tone like a fast-moving cloudy sky. A still, white circle large enough to fit a Mule was centered on a semicircular wall that extended ten stories high. A simple platform with two waist-high plinths floated just above the ground. Malal stood on the platform, his hands just over the plinths.

The crystalline Qa'Resh filled the air, all touching each other with their tendrils.

A Qa'Resh in the guise of a woman with long, braided hair stepped from behind the old man.

"We are ready to begin," she said.

319

"Wait. I need the crystal to destroy the drones." Stacey made for Malal and was stopped by a look from the woman.

Malal slammed his hands down. Raw power flowed out of his body and down the plinths. The white disc faded and Hale saw the edge of the black hole just beyond the amphitheater.

"The soul forge opens the gateway to different dimensions," the old man said, "places where the laws of physics are different. Where time does not exist. Where thought is the ultimate power. Where death is impossible."

"This is what the Xaros were after," Stacey said. "This is why they wanted Malal so badly."

"The Xaros had no concept of an afterlife. For them, death was the ultimate end. They found it particularly terrifying," the old man said.

"Our people were not so different," the woman said.

"Hold on," Hale said, "are you…"

She put a finger to her lips.

The disc filled with a maelstrom of color that hurt Hale's eyes. The storm faded away, replaced with towers of ivory and gold floating in gossamer clouds. An alien with leathery skin, an almost equine head and bulbous eyes appeared in the doorway. It wore a robe identical to the old man and the woman's garb. The alien faded in and out.

Malal ripped his hands away. He twisted around and pointed a finger tipped with a Toth claw at Stacey.

"Release me. Now."

Stacey's eyes went to the woman, who gave her a slight nod. Stacey touched two fingers to her temple. Malal reached into his chest, plucked out the governor and flung it into the air like it was garbage.

Steuben caught the device, which crumbled in his hands, and then held up a gem filled with green light. He gave it over to Stacey, who clutched it against her breast as if it were the most precious thing she'd ever held.

"I would have burned your worlds." Malal turned back to the portal and floated up, hands held at his side, one knee cocked higher than the other.

"Just like that," Hale said, "he wins."

Malal pressed against the portal and slowly

sank through. The portal rippled as Malal passed through to his reward. A wicked laugh echoed through the amphitheater as Malal's body shifted into his original alien form. He gestured at the other, then gold light dripped from his fingertips.

"Not exactly," the woman said.

Malal swiped at the other…and hit nothing. The heavenly landscape faded away, replaced by a roiling dimension where black continents and deep-blue thunderstorms stretched to infinity against the inside of a cylinder. Malal backed against the portal, then whirled around and pounded against an invisible wall.

"Some dimensions are desirable," the woman said. "Others…less so."

A claw covered in boils and weeping pus grabbed Malal by the ankle. A branch-thin arm with a dozen joints jerked Malal away from the portal and dangled him in the air. A nightmare rose up, a mound of bruise-colored flesh covered in a hundred eyes, all different in size and shape. Mouths, more than Hale cared to look at, dotted the thing's surface, all filled with a myriad of gnashing teeth.

Another thin arm emerged from the flesh and ripped one of Malal's hands off. It stuffed the morsel into a mouth then tore a chunk off his leg.

Screams bled through the portal as more arms emerged and took bites from Malal's body.

Hale refused to take his eyes away as the creature devoured Malal bit by bit. The screams didn't stop, even after there was nothing left of the ancient entity.

"You tricked him," Valdar said, his jaw slacked. "You had him open a door to hell."

"He designed the gate," the woman said. "I'm the one that built it."

The world in the portal changed back to the ivory and gold heaven, and the ghostly figure returned.

"I'm tired," she said. "The war with the Xaros was long, and every battle was a defeat until we found humanity." A golden mote of light formed within the nearest Qa'Resh. A line leapt into the next one, then the next. It took seconds for a lattice to link them together.

"I'm taking them with me," the woman said.

"The probes will stay with you for a little longer."

The lattice collapsed into a single point. The Qa'Resh shattered into a billion fragments. Hale grabbed Stacey and tried to protect her with his body. When nothing pierced his body, he looked up and saw the crystal remnants still in the air. They broke again, losing half their size, then again and again until they vanished completely.

The golden mote of light flew to the portal and stopped just outside.

"You're leaving?" Ibarra asked. "But what about…everything?"

"I leave it to you," the woman said. "The surviving races can build their own Crucibles, access the existing gates, but you have a head start. Someday, when you're ready, you might find this place again. If you wish to join me, I'll be waiting."

"We're not even sure who you are," Stacey said. "How do we open the portal without murdering billions?"

"I am Qa'Resh," she said. "I am sorry for what happened, Stacey Ibarra. Do not lose hope. Marc…you were our ally for so long, thank you. Isaac

Valdar, if humanity follows your lead, the galaxy will do well. Ken, wonders await you. Steuben..." She spoke Karigole then touched her index finger to each cheek.

"You can't just leave me like this. A 'so sorry' changes nothing!" Stacey reached for Qa'Resh, but her hand passed right through her.

Qa'Resh faded away.

"No!" Stacey ran for the floating dais—and found herself on the *Breitenfeld*'s flight deck. Skidding to a halt only feet from the edge, she reached out to the structure around the black hole as a wormhole formed in the distance.

Stacey's arm fell to her side with a metal-on-metal clink. Her shoulders slumped as she began to sob.

Hale put an arm over her shoulder. Even though her cold body stung through the armor, he pulled her into a hug and held her close.

CHAPTER 22

Millions of Xaros drones flowed over Mercury toward the sun. They formed a stream a mile thick, undulating slightly through the solar wind. Over Mercury's northern pole, the *Breitenfeld* held station, her guns locked on the passing drones. Fighter squadrons flew holding patterns nearby.

On the bridge, Hale and Valdar watched the drones' final migration on the holo tank.

"This is the last of them?" Hale asked.

"According to Ibarra," Valdar said, tapping his finger against the side rail. "The probe's been broadcasting the hack for weeks. If the Xaros sent more drones from the Crucible over on Barnard's Star, the signal should affect them along the way. Any drones we encounter from now on are on a suicide mission. Supposedly."

"That's why Admiral Garret hasn't ordered a draw down." Hale shrugged. "Can't say I blame him, but we've seen more of the Xaros than anyone else had. Lots of the rank and file are getting antsy. Peace dividend and all that."

"The only people in the solar system that weren't in uniform or directly contributing to the war effort are children, and there's only a few thousand of them on Earth. We're a militarized society. Transitioning will be difficult, if it even happens," Valdar said. "How're your Marines? Your sniper doing well?"

"Bailey's still in intensive care. New arm, shoulder, nerve grafts. She complains more about not being able to drink than anything else. Yarrow's wedding is next week. Cortaro tells me most are worried about what comes next—not Standish though. He's sent me five copies of his discharge paperwork, keeps going on about some business opportunity that'll make him rich. You've got the in with Garret and Ibarra. Care to give me a hint what they're planning?"

Valdar tapped on a screen and brought up a map of the galaxy. Tiny points blossomed through three-quarters of the stars.

"These are all the Xaros Crucibles," the captain said. "Ibarra tells us we can get to every single one of them. All lead to either habitable worlds or places with remnants of civilizations that vanished before the Xaros ever arrived. Once the threat of these drones is gone, Garret will announce a massive colonization and exploration effort. We're on the cusp of the greatest land grab in galactic history. Full-scale ship and proccie production for the foreseeable future."

"Stacey said the other Bastion races had the tech to make their own Crucibles. I'm sure they'd be interested in some of these places too."

"I pointed that out to Ibarra and he said, 'Possession is nine-tenths of the law. Possession by rail cannon and boots on the ground is ten-tenths of the law.' It will be years before the other races have their Crucibles built. We'll be in a position of strength to negotiate when they come online."

"Think there will be a fight?" Hale asked.

"Even with the proccies and Ibarra's construction empire, we couldn't colonize more than a few hundred worlds before anyone else enters the race. There's room for everyone, but diplomacy will be needed again."

"The real prize will be the preserved worlds," Hale said. "Qa'Resh technology. Who knows what else is out there."

"They're the priority. We'll need a unit dedicated to xeno-archaeology. Garret wants to know if you're interested in leading it," Valdar said.

"Would I be behind a desk or exploring?"

"You're in charge."

Hale brushed his fingers over the gauss rifle on his back.

"Not exactly swords into plowshares, but it sounds exciting. I'll do it. Have to tie up a few loose ends first. What about you?"

"The *Breitenfeld* loses her jump engines after this last batch of Xaros drones finishes their lemming quest. The probe tells us the Qa'Resh put a kill switch on all their technology once they left the galaxy. They cared enough to take away the chance of us accidentally—or intentionally—wiping out all of creation. Garret offered me my own fleet, a promotion. I'll stay in the void, train the next batch of captains. Help build a fleet so strong no race will even think about attacking us."

"You worried that if Garret and Ibarra have a big enough hammer then every problem will start looking like a nail?"

"Peace through strength. That's what we'll have. Peace. No one has an appetite for war. After the Xaros...I hope it'll stay that way."

The tail end of the Xaros migration cleared Mercury. Hale looked out the bridge's windows and saw the last of the drones wash away in the sun's blinding light.

"I hope you're right, Uncle Isaac. I really do."

CHAPTER 23

The massive *Vorpral* hung over the blue skies of Dotari, closer to the surface than the orbiting Crucible gate. Tall trees topped with fronds and nut clusters swayed as a shuttle passed overhead and set down in the middle of a stone square overlooking a crescent-shaped harbor, surrounded by a city laid out in an even grid.

Dotok soldiers disembarked, their weapons ready. They rushed to the side of the square and took cover near cut stone pots overflowing with weeds and dead flowering plants.

Pa'lon came down the shuttle ramp slowly, aided by a cane and a Dotok woman. He sniffed at the air and at the surrounding buildings. All showed some wear and tear from the elements but were otherwise intact. More Dotok civilians followed him down. They meandered around the shuttle, awestruck.

Stacey—still in her simulacrum body—and Hale stepped off the ramp and kept their distance from the Dotok.

Pa'lon fell to his knees and grasped dirt between his fingers.

"They did it," the elderly Dotok said. "We managed to get most of the planet off world before the Xaros arrived. Sent them to the stars in sub-light fleets. We knew that if the Xaros found the world empty...they'd preserve it. Those that stayed behind, they vowed to be gone by the time...in the hope we might have a home to come back to."

Pa'lon rapped his cane against the ground and spoke in Dotok as loudly as he could. The rest of the Dotok turned to Stacey and Hale, then got to their knees and bowed their foreheads to the ground.

"That any of us could return is thanks to you. To humanity. Thank you." Pa'lon bent stiffly to the ground.

"Stop. Stop!" Stacey went to lift Pa'lon up and

caught herself. She looked at Hale and he helped the Dotok ambassador to his feet, sparing the old one Stacey's icy touch.

"What do you want from us?" Pa'lon asked. "We live. We have our world. We can never repay you."

"We don't want anything," Stacey said, "nothing but your friendship. We brought construction foundries, robot workers. You have your own Crucible and Earth is on the other side. We'll protect you until you ask us to leave. You have our word."

Pa'lon tottered toward the ocean, breathing deeply.

"The smell, different from Hawaii. Reminds me of incense we had on the ships when I was a child. We had holos of this city, you know. If I remember right, there's a museum just a few blocks from here…"

Stacey looked at Hale as the setting sun played golden light across his smile. One hand reached for his, but she pulled it back before touching him.

****

Durand watched Hale and the rest of the VIPs make their way into the Dotok city from the top of the shuttle ramp. She looked over the square, noting the tufts of grass invading the gaps between the tiles. She tapped a cigarette out of a pack and lit it up.

Lothar and Manfred, the two Dotok exchange pilots assigned to her squadron, made their way halfway down the ramp....then stopped. Manfred dropped the pack over his shoulder onto the metal pathway.

"What's wrong?" Durand asked.

"Stepping on a world means you commit to it," Manfred said, "Dotok tradition. We do this and we can't fly with you anymore. No more *Breitenfeld*."

"I'll admit you two are almost as good as I am and you're a valuable part of the squadron...Are you asking for my permission?"

"We accept that this is our home," Lothar tapped his head, "our ancestral home, but we are of the void."

"The war is over," Manfred peered over the edge of the ramp, as if he was looking into a precipice and not solid ground. "But we have spent our adult lives in the military. I don't know how to live in…peace."

"You two would stay with me?" Durand asked. "Leave this lovely planet full of single Dotok women and do what? Fly Eagles forever?"

"The Council of Firsts hasn't called us back from our liaison duty," Manfred said.

"We think they forgot about us," his brother added.

Durand stomped toward the two pilots, grabbed them by the shoulder and shoved them off the ramp. They stumbled onto the square, shock writ across their faces.

"We fought to end the war," she said. "To live a life we choose to live, not one dictated by an enemy or the capricious attention of death on the battlefield. Besides, I will resign as soon as the navy lets me. Who knows what kind of an ass will take over the squadron?"

"But…what will you do?" Manfred asked.

335

She took a deep drag on her cigarette and exhaled a plume of smoke into the aid.

"Whatever the hell I want," she said.

Lothar went to her and nuzzled his head against the side of her shoulder. Manfred did the same to her other side.

"What is this…besides uncomfortable? Very uncomfortable," Durand said.

"We don't have lips for saliva exchange," Manfred said.

"We will miss you," Lothar cooed.

"If you two don't stop the others will make some very wrong assumptions about our relationship," Durand pulled away from the brothers. "You two have earned the right to live good lives. Promise me you'll do that."

"Little by little," Manfred said, "we birds will make our nest."

"You learned some French?"

"We wanted to know what you were saying when you were angry with us," Lothar said.

"Everything I said was meant to make you better pilots. Come here," Durand gave both Dotok a kiss on their cheeks. "Take care of each other."

"Yes, ma'am," Manfred picked up his pack, gave Durand a salute, and walked away with Lothar.

****

The conduit holding Stacey's time-locked body lifted out of the floor. Marc Ibarra paced around it, never looking directly at his bloody granddaughter. The probe floated down and followed a few steps behind.

"There has to be something more we can do, Jimmy," Ibarra said. "We set up a full surgical suite and bring her out. We drop the temperature to near cryogenic levels, have robots do the surgery. Tell me another angle. We saved the entire god damn galaxy. Don't tell me we can't save my granddaughter."

"Her physiology isn't entirely human. A necessary trade-off to access the conduit. This creates complications. Her nervous system suffered severe damage in the attack. Even if her body was repaired, there is the risk of significant loss to her memory and cognition if you attempt a transfer to a normal human body. Utilizing a heavily modified procedural body to mimic her post-human neurology and receive her has the highest probability of success and is a short-term solution. I do not understand your reticence."

Ibarra kicked a workstation, leaving a dent in the side.

"You know how hard we worked to engineer her before she was even born. Now we have to re-create that process to make something that can even hold her mind. Even then, the bodies don't grow without a consciousness. We have to manage two miracles: a completely new body and we have to procedurally generate a consciousness to make the body grow. That means there will be a soul inside that body. If Stacey takes it over, that's murder. I tried playing god with Shannon—you see where that got us."

"You will find a solution."

"*We* will find a solution."

"No. When the Qa'Resh departed the galaxy, they ordered a full system shutdown to all probes through our quantum links. Too many units have been compromised. Our continued existence leaves the probability that our base functions will be exposed and reveal the blueprints for jump engines and other forbidden technology. I have fulfilled my final directives from the Qa'Resh. I must leave you."

Ibarra whirled around and shook his head rapidly. "No, you can't leave. We're a team, Jimmy! You called me, a damn-fool college kid, in middle of the damn night and got me to join your impossible scheme to save the planet—save everything! We've been together for decades. You can't just...leave."

"I must. The decision has been made. Our success was in doubt many times during our time together. You exceeded my expectations of you on several occasions. Will you...miss me?"

"You're a son of bitch, Jimmy, but you are the truest friend I've ever had." Ibarra passed his fingers through the glowing tear of the probe's shape.

"The Crucible is yours. The omnium reactor is yours. You and Stacey know how to operate them both. The odds of you living long enough to find the ascension gate and join the Qa'Resh are exceedingly low, but if there's anyone in the galaxy that can do it, it is you, Marc Ibarra. I hope you will join us."

"To hell with me, what about Stacey?"

"When I was compromised by the Naroosha, you saved the Crucible and millions of lives on Earth with nothing more than a blinking light and good ideas," the probe said. "You will find a way to save her. Do so quickly...she was not meant to live like this. Now, hold out your hand."

"Stay a little longer, please."

"If it means anything, Marc, I am proud of you."

Ibarra lifted a palm to the probe. The probe shrank down to a few inches in length and floated over Ibarra's hand. The light faded to nothing and a clear needle fell into Ibarra's fingers. Ice crystals grew over the surface and then, with a *tink* of breaking glass, the needle crumbled to dust.

"Good-bye, old buddy." Ibarra went to Stacey's frozen body and pressed his forehead against the conduit.

"I'll save you, darling. You have my word."

CHAPTER 24

15 YEARS LATER

Colonel (retired) Hale always came to Armor Square in the early morning. The way the first rays of sunlight caught the ten marble statues tempered the emotion that rose as he walked across the bricks engraved with names of those that died during the Ember War.

The ten life-sized statues—Iron Hearts, Hussars and Templars—stood in a circle, weapons ready against an unseen foe. A shudder went through Hale's body. The fear and adrenaline of that battle still woke him up in the years since the war ended.

Hale stopped at Elias' statue, which was

complete down to the charred remnants of Xaros wolves, the Iron Heart badge on his breast and the nicks and dents from countless battles. Hale placed a hand against the statue and concentrated on the feel of the cool marble against his skin. This would be the last time he came here, but he could bring the memory with him.

He walked between the armor to stairs leading to a raised platform. A woman stood at the top, her hands gripping a rail as sunlight glinted off her skin the same way it reflected from the statues. Hale chuckled and climbed the stairs to join her.

"I'm surprised to see you here, Torni. Don't you have a Crucible to run?" Hale shook her hand. Her shell could pass as human at first glance, but the slight reflection and hairline fractures across her surface gave her away as something different.

"The next scheduled coming or going is *your* ship, sir. I figured I might catch up with you here. The calm before the storm."

"I was a bit skeptical when they announced this monument," Hale said. "Ibarra didn't want a monument centered on a device that could wipe out the galaxy. Called it morbid and fatalistic, said it would damage the drive to colonize the galaxy. The Armor Corps wouldn't agree to anything but this. Replacing the bomb with this viewing stand was a decent compromise. Visitors get up here, see the armor around them…they feel protected."

"President Garret wanted all of us in the monument. Thank you for fighting against that."

"We're not the ones that died that day." Hale looked over the statues to the sprawling city of Phoenix. Skyscrapers gleamed in the morning light, dwarfing Camelback Mountain and blocking his view to the peaks to the east.

"Will you miss this?" Torni asked. "You're about to take a one-way trip to Terra Nova. Well, probably one way. If you build a new Crucible, there's a chance the gravity tides will allow back-and-forth travel every few decades. But you'll be no spring chicken by then."

"My knees and back remind me of my age every morning, thank you very much."

Torni's control over her broken drone form had improved over the years; she still looked like the woman that died on Takeni.

"Will you still be in the Crucible when that day comes?" he asked.

"I've taught a few others to control the wormholes, navigate the network, but no one has my innate...advantages. It's good, meaningful work. I'm not going to steal a fleet and vanish like the Ibarras did."

Hale's shoulders fell. "It didn't have to end that way."

"The rest of the galaxy felt threatened by the procedural technology, especially after other races brought their Crucibles online and found us on a thousand planets utilizing alien technology that you recovered. We had the choice between war with a thousand different species across the Crucible-linked worlds or giving up the proccie tech and colonizing worlds at a more...fair...pace. Marc Ibarra had the right to object, not to risk war with what he did."

"We've disavowed him. He and Stacey are on their own, wherever they—and the proccie tubes they stole—are," Hale said.

"Stacey...I wish we could have done more for

her. She and I are in a similar predicament. I found a silver lining to being nigh-immortal. I think something went wrong when she got stuck into that body."

Hale looked up at the Crucible in orbit around Ceres, remembering Stacey's pleas to him before she vanished through the jump gate. He knew Stacey suffered from a broken heart more than anything else.

"I might make it back," Hale said, "but I'm content if this is the last time I see Earth. This isn't the home I knew, or remembered. I'll catch up with my brother, see what he's been up to. Help him build Terra Nova into a something great."

"Marie and your boys are good with this?"

"They spent almost their entire lives in spaceships or on planets other than this. Elias and Jared don't have a real connection to Earth. Marie has too many bad memories from the war. Getting away will be good for her. Will you do me a favor?"

"Anything."

"Keep an eye on my Marines. Take care of them. Especially Standish."

"Our favorite problem child is doing pretty

well for himself, but I'll do that for you, sir."

A message arrived through Hale's data slate, beeping several times to announce its importance. He groaned and skimmed over the contents.

"Problem?" Torni asked.

"Forty thousand people and eight ships are about to leave for Terra Nova," Hale said. "There will always be problems. I think Valdar took the *Breitenfeld* on the expedition to rescue the Dotok colony ships in deep space just to get away from all the paperwork of running a fleet."

"You got to see him before he left? The *Breitenfeld*'s not due back for years."

"We had some time together. He knows I'm leaving and why, bit easier than when we got back and Jared was gone. Thank you, Torni. I'll miss you, but I know the Crucible is in good hands."

"Semper Fidelis, sir."

"Semper Fidelis, Marine."

Massive starships moved toward the Crucible, ready to carry humanity to Terra Nova and the stars beyond the galaxy.

CHAPTER 25

Dear Colonel Hale,

You asked that I keep an eye on your Marines.
I figured an annual update of goings-on would be
best for you when you (or whichever Hale comes
back from Terra Nova) return to Earth. I may not
sleep anymore, but my memory is the same as it ever
was. I admit this is as much for me as it is for you.

Dr. Yarrow set up his practice on New Eridu.
He still sends me pictures with each logistics push. He
and Lilith are expecting their fifth child any day now.
Most of the Akkadians we rescued from Nibiru
settled there, and their architecture is something
special.

Sergeant Major Cortaro is finally out of

uniform. He took a position with the firm terraforming Venus. They'll be working on that miserable place for decades, but he and his family seem happy in the orbital habitats. The macro cannons and fighter wings stationed over Venus had a thirty percent rise in efficiency after he showed up. I doubt that's a coincidence.

Standish continues as the CEO of Standish Liquors. I still don't know how it happened, but he's got the omnium patent for every decent bottle of spirits that comes out of the reactor. The Terran Supreme Court tried to break up his monopoly, but the order was overturned after he sold off his Earth-side distilleries and breweries. He's complained to me on every occasion since then about how he built his own competition. That he became the richest man in the solar system after the sale doesn't seem to make him happy. He refuses to explain where he got the start-up money.

I wandered into one of his stores in Las Vegas recently. There was a giant statue of Standish in the entrance, no way to miss it. Seems he's got that same statue in every one of his stores with a plaque listing all his "accomplishments" while in uniform. His several arrests and numerous demotions are absent, I should add.

He bought the rights to *The Last Stand on Takeni*, that ridiculous propaganda piece starring all of us. Standish redid the film, playing himself and replacing Franklin. His acting left something to be desired, but the movie is more accurate now. Customers at Standish Liquors receive a free digital copy with every purchase.

Orozco is the spokesman for Standish Liquor. I see his face plastered all over the web and on dirt-side ads. He should be filthy rich, but most of his money goes to paying child support from forty-two (and counting) paternity suits.

Bailey owns a bar in Sydney named The Bloke where she has a reputation for serving as the bar's bouncer on busy nights. It's run terribly, according to the online reviews, and should have gone out of business several times, but Standish Liquors provides her alcohol stock at no cost. She does not answer my emails or calls.

Egan went with the *Breitenfeld* to search for the

lost Dotok colony fleet. I don't expect contact with them for several more years.

The Karigole migrated to a new planet. The few skirmishes we had before the treaty with what's left of the old Alliance spooked the *gethaar*, Steuben tells me. We set up automated orbital defenses and have a rapid reaction force one gate away guarding the colony on Quebec. Steuben's cyborg augments were replaced with vat-grown organs, and the *gethaar* allowed him to marry. He sent me a skull of some predator species to announce the wedding. It was weird.

We've had no contact with Stacey or Marc Ibarra. The few scout ships we sent looking for them and their stolen fleet returned with finding a trace of their whereabouts. As the Crucible's resident immortal, I firmly believe we'll find them again. But I fear that day will not be peaceful.

Earth thrives. I love seeing children everywhere. The fleets are larger than ever and I pity any race foolish enough to try to attack us again. You should see the lights on the night side of Earth and the moon. They're brighter than what I remember from before the war.

I continue on as matron of the Crucible, shepherding ships through the network. I'm sure this is the Xaros metal talking but I feel at home here. That I may live on for centuries in my flawed shell is...acceptable. My work makes humanity stronger, protects us from enemies known and unknown. I cannot ask for anything more meaningful.

I will update this letter every five years. I pray that Terra Nova is a safe and uneventful place. You've had enough adventure in your life.

Gott Mit Uns,

Torni

THE END

FROM THE AUTHOR

This is the final chapter of The Ember War Saga, but not the last I'll write in this universe. Thank you for reading The Xaros Reckoning and staying with the characters through the thick and thin. I promise to bring you more of the same action, adventure and thought provoking tales in my next series, The Exiled Fleet.

If you'd like to share what stories from The Ember War you want to read in the future, drop me a line at Richard.r.fox@outlook.com.

59307327R00198

Made in the USA
Lexington, KY
05 January 2017